DEAD END

TYNDALE HOUSE PUBLISHERS, INC., CAROL STREAM, ILLINOIS

RED ROCK MYSTERIES

#1 BEST-SELLING AUTHORS

JERRY B. JENKINS · CHRIS FABRY

Visit Tyndale's exciting Web site for kids at cool2read.com
Also see the Web site for adults at tyndale.com

Dead End

Designed by Jacqueline L. Noe
Edited by Lorie Popp

Published in association with the literary agency of Alive Communications, Inc., 7680 Goddard Street, Suite 200, Colorado Springs, CO 80920.

Library of Congress Cataloging-in-Publication Data

Jenkins, Jerry B.
Dead end / Jerry B. Jenkins ; Chris Fabry.
p. cm. — (Red Rock mysteries ; 15)
Summary: Twins Ashley and Bryce face their toughest challenge yet when the terrorist responsible for their father's death seeks revenge against their stepfather, a government agent, and targets schools, beginning with theirs.
ISBN-13: 978-1-4143-0154-9 (pbk.)
ISBN-10: 1-4143-0154-5 (pbk.)
[1. Terrorism—Fiction. 2. Schools—Fiction. 3. Christian life—Fiction. 4. Twins—Fiction. 5. Colorado—Fiction. 6. Mystery and detective stories.] I. Fabry, Chris, date. II. Title. III. Series: Jenkins, Jerry B. Red Rock mysteries ; 15.
PZ7.J4138Ddw 2006
[Fic]—dc22 2006009257

Printed in the United States of America

09 08 07 06
9 8 7 6 5 4 3 2 1

To Reagan Fabry

"If by my life or death
I can protect you, I will."

Aragorn

"To finish is a sadness to a writer—
a little death. He puts the LAST word down
and it is done. But it isn't really done.
The story goes on and leaves the writer
behind, for no story is ever done."

John Steinbeck

"So don't worry about tomorrow,
for tomorrow will bring its own worries.
Today's trouble is enough for today."

Jesus, Matthew 6:34

BEFORE

RED RIVER, TEXAS

The man had dark bronze skin, as if he had spent a year at the beach. His eyebrows were thick, and his black hair was cut close. He wore a black jacket and jeans and walked like a lion, strutting into the underground compound.

People stood when he entered. They had waited for this moment, worked toward it.

"Sit," Dark Man said.

All obeyed, as they would a king.

He walked to a table filled with fruit, picked up an apple, and began eating. His gaze ran around the room methodically, analyzing each person. "Have the preparations been made?"

A short, bald man leaned forward, nervously twirling a pencil. "Sir, we've notified the cells that you are here, and Operation Hamar is ready—"

"How many schools?" Dark Man interrupted.

The bald man handed a folder to him. "Fifteen in the Midwest. Twelve in the East. Ten in the West. All of the attacks will be coordinated, so the authorities will not have time—"

Dark Man raised a hand and closed the folder. "You have information on the man I seek?"

The bald man glanced at a woman across the table. An American. Short brown hair. She stood before she spoke as a sign of courtesy. "Sir, we've matched two children in Colorado with the identity of the previous target."

"Timberline?"

"Yes. As you believed, the agent was never on the plane. When it was destroyed, he went into hiding, assuming a new identity."

Dark Man opened another folder and studied a picture—a mustached American in cowboy boots and a denim jacket. "Samuel Timberline," he hissed.

"He married the widow of a businessman on the plane. He has an older daughter by his first wife and is stepfather to three."

"A family of six." Dark Man laughed. "Convenient."

"He is a charter pilot," the woman continued. "He lives in that house; his wife is a writer. We know his schedule. We know everything."

He tossed the apple core and slammed the folder on the table. "Where?"

She opened a map and pointed. "The town is called Red Rock."

"You have made their school a target?"

The woman smiled and nodded.

Dark Man sat and leaned forward, elbows on the table. “We have waited to show America our power. Now we will strike where they are most vulnerable.” He pounded a finger on the picture of Sam Timberline. “I will coordinate the initial strike in Colorado. And I promise you, this man and his family will be the first to die.”

PART 1

CHAPTER 1

THREE WEEKS UNTIL THE END OF SCHOOL

❀ Ashley ❀

Eighth grade is supposed to be the highlight of middle school, but it's been a mixed bag for Bryce and me. He's my younger twin brother—I'm older by 57 seconds. We've had victories in speech tournaments, and Bryce had a good basketball season, but a lot of bad things have happened with our friends.

Bryce and his friend Kael aren't talking. My best friend, Hayley, got mad because I've spent time with Marion Quidley. Marion asked a lot of questions about God, but she hasn't become a Christian. I wonder if she ever will.

School is winding down—only three weeks until the eighth-grade dance and summer, and the beginning of ninth grade is just around the corner. They called us "pixies" in sixth grade. I wonder if "freshmen" will be worse at Red Rock High.

The best thing about the past few weeks has been our writing contest. It promises great prizes and guarantees at least one winner per school, so a lot of kids have entered.

We were eating dinner early that Sunday because Pastor Andy was picking Bryce and me up for some volunteer work. Leigh, our older stepsister, came running in crying. It wasn't the kind of thing you see in the movies, where a girl makes a big scene and wails like a police siren. I could just tell by the way she didn't look at us as she passed.

Dylan, our little brother who's finishing kindergarten, bit into his meat loaf and spit it out. "Hot!" he said.

"Blow on it," Mom said, putting her napkin down and following Leigh.

Bryce doused Dylan's meat loaf with ketchup.

"Can you mash my potato?" Dylan called after Mom.

"Here, I'll do it," I said. His potato was cut in half, and a river of butter ran through it. I used a fork to mash it, but I got potato skin mixed in, which he doesn't like. "Try your corn," I said.

"I don't like corn. It makes me toot."

Bryce snickered.

Mom came back and settled Dylan down with a cup of lemonade. Then he cried because he didn't want to look at the meat loaf he'd spit out, and I couldn't blame him.

"When is Sam coming home?" I asked Mom. He and Mom are okay with us calling him that because he's our stepdad.

"He's still in DC. I'm not sure when he'll be back."

"What's going on?" Bryce said.

She sighed, and I could tell that she knew more than she was saying. "It's an alert. They asked him to look at some Internet messages—chatter, he calls it."

"What's wrong upstairs?" I said, changing the subject.

She gave me a worried look. "I'm not sure."

Dylan dropped a hunk of meat loaf into his corn, and he cried so hard it sounded like someone had chopped off his ears.

Pippin barked at the front door, and Bryce and I jumped.

"That's Pastor Andy," he said. "See you, Mom."

CHAPTER 2

Bryce

Pastor Andy has been leading the youth group at church for almost five years, which is a lifetime for a youth pastor. He does a lot with the senior high kids, and his wife has called Leigh a couple of times, but that's pretty much like asking a snowman to go tanning.

He drove the church's van, and there were a couple of older kids inside who acted like Ashley and I were nuisances. Andy asked us how we were doing and about school. He mentioned Leigh, and I told him that she still didn't want anything to do with church.

"Too bad," he said. "I was hoping with what's going on . . . well, I had hoped she'd change her mind."

"What's going on?" Ashley said.

Andy blushed. "I . . . uh, can't really talk about it."

I looked at Ashley as Andy launched into a description of our jobs. The youth group mows yards for old people and picks up trash along the highway. At Christmas, Ashley and I babysat for a woman whose husband died. It was sad, but Ashley and I knew what those kids were going through. The first Christmas without Dad was the worst.

"The old place we're working on used to be a school and I think a government building at one point," Pastor Andy said.

"What are they doing to it?" I said.

"It's going to be an orphanage. The Chapmans are renovating it. They're the ones with all the foster kids. The place has nine bedrooms, but it's trashed right now."

"What's our job?" Ashley said.

"We're cleaning so they can paint. The basement will be more of a challenge. I was hoping you two could handle that."

We parked behind a brick building that looked like a fire station. It had a huge archway in front and some broken windows on the third floor. Hammers pounded inside, and a radio blasted a Christian group.

"What do you think Andy knows about Leigh?" I said as we walked to the basement.

Ashley shrugged.

CHAPTER 3

❀ Ashley ❀

Bryce and I put on gloves and little white masks so we wouldn't breathe too much dust. Our first task was to haul dusty boxes outside to a huge trash bin.

I'd seen the Chapmans in church. The mom and dad couldn't have children, so they tried adoption. When that fell through they took in a foster child. A second one came, and soon they had a lot of kids.

After an hour of hauling, the basement looked better. We found a huge fireplace, and I imagined a Ping-Pong table, couches, and a big TV down there.

Pastor Andy checked our progress and looked impressed. He held up his watch and said, "You probably won't be able to finish, but up next is the ceiling. We need to tear it out."

Bryce and I removed crumbling tiles that looked like chalk. Many were water damaged and fell apart. I stood on a stepladder, Bryce on a chair, and we threw the tiles in a corner. When we had a tall stack, we'd dump them in the bin and brush the dust from our hair.

We were halfway through with the main section when something tumbled out of the ceiling.

Bryce held it up. "Ash, it's a wallet."

CHAPTER 4

Bryce

The wallet looked a hundred years old and was crumbling. I opened it, my hands shaking. There was nothing green inside, just some faded pictures, a Social Security card, and an old key. I read the name to Ashley.

She shook her head. "Never heard of him."

I stuffed the wallet in my pocket and worked on the next panel. Four more wallets fell out. A piece of paper stuck out of one. It was a pamphlet folded in half that talked about the best way to survive an atomic bomb.

"Ash, these have been here a long time."

Pastor Andy came back, and we showed him the wallets. There was no money in any of them, but there were old letters, driver's licenses, snapshots, and one even had a ring. We found 12 wallets in all.

Andy looked them over. "You two are good at mysteries. How do you think they got up there?"

I looked at my sister. "You go first."

Ashley scratched her head. "The ceiling is low, so somebody tall could have stolen them and stashed them there."

"That would explain why there's no money in them," I said. "What should we do with them?"

"Take them and I'll talk with the Chapmans," Andy said.

We put the wallets in a garbage bag. I wondered if the memories in them were more than just trash.

CHAPTER 5

❀ Ashley ❀

Bryce and I rode our bikes to school the next day. I saw a friend by the bike rack and talked. We lost track of time, and I was late to first period. Not a good start to the day. Plus, Marion Quidley saw me and kept walking.

When I went to get my lunch, an envelope fell out of my locker. A bustling crowd passed as I stooped to get it. It had my name written on the front in red ink.

Strange.

I opened it carefully and found an expensive card with a picture of a single rose on the front. My heart skipped a beat.

"What's up?" someone said behind me.

I shoved the card under some books and turned. It was Marion.

"Nothing," I said. "You going to lunch?"

"Thought I'd eat outside. It's a little windy, but I sit behind the climbing wall."

"I'll join you," I said, grabbing the bag I had packed this morning.

Once Bryce and I graduated from elementary school, Mom made us pack our own lunches. She supplied ham or turkey or peanut butter and jelly, along with chips and snacks. She said if we were old enough to drive ATVs, we were old enough to make our own lunches.

The sunshine was almost blinding as we walked outside, and it made me think of Bryce. He loves watching the Cubs or the Rockies—just the sight of grass growing and sunshine makes him pine for baseball.

Marion didn't say anything as she opened her organic-yogurt container and a bag of whole-wheat crackers. Her family doesn't have much money, but somehow she always comes to school with the healthiest food.

"Guess you're wondering where I'm at with the God thing," Marion said, licking her plastic spoon.

I was really thinking about the card in my locker, but I nodded. We'd had a good talk in Tres Peaks, and she seemed interested in spiritual stuff.

She crunched a few crackers. "Remember what you said after I gave my speech?"

I shook my head.

"I asked, what if God hadn't answered my prayer about going to the tournament? What if someone hadn't paid the money?"

It was coming back. Marion had made a bargain with God—that

if he let her go to the tournament, she would read the Bible. "You've got a new problem?" I said.

"A long time ago I prayed about my dad's health. Why would God answer a prayer about a dumb old speech tournament and keep my dad sick?"

I opened my peanut-butter-and-jelly sandwich and tried to think of an answer.

CHAPTER 6

Bryce

At lunch I looked for Ashley but couldn't find her. I ate fast and walked into the courtyard. It was a gorgeous day, perfect baseball weather, and the wind was blowing toward the fences. The Cubs were playing in St. Louis tonight.

I pulled out my cell phone and dialed the Chapmans' number. Pastor Andy had talked with Mom and told her the Chapmans didn't know anything about the wallets. I wanted to ask some questions myself and had looked up their number before we left the house. Mrs. Chapman answered and gave me her husband's work number.

I called him and told him about the wallets.

"Yeah, Andy told me about your find," Mr. Chapman said. "Any money inside?"

"Mostly licenses and stuff. I'm wondering if you know about the building's history."

"The previous owners were young. They had it only a year and gave up on turning it into a restaurant. Sorry."

"Anybody else who might know?"

He paused. "I know a collector who keeps up with the history of the town."

"What's his name?"

"Bob Gerrill."

The name rang a bell, but I couldn't place it. It wasn't until I found a local phone directory that I put it together. I had talked with him after some of his Civil War artifacts were stolen. I dialed his number and asked if I could stop by after school.

"Sure, Bryce. I'd love to see you again."

CHAPTER 7

❀ Ashley ❀

I wished Pastor Andy were here or that I could give Marion a book or a tape, but she was looking at me with hungry eyes. It's funny that you can pray for someone, and then when they get interested in God and ask questions, you panic.

"When you mentioned your bargain, it kind of made me nervous because some people treat God like a genie. You ask for stuff and rub the lamp, and he gives it. The problem comes when he doesn't give what you want."

"You think I think God is a genie?"

"No, I didn't mean it that way—"

"Because you act like you know everything, Ashley."

I couldn't speak. Her words were like daggers. Someone once said that telling a person about Jesus is like a beggar telling another beggar where to find bread. The beggar beside me wasn't happy with the directions.

"You asked me a question," I said. "I *don't* know all the answers. But I do know that God loves you and wants the best for you."

"Then why did he let my dad get sick? If Jesus can raise the dead and stop a big storm, why wouldn't he do this for me?"

"Let's back up. Do you believe there's a God?"

"I don't know anymore."

My heart dropped. I'd pictured Marion going to church with us. Mom had talked about starting a Bible study at our house for girls my age, and I hoped Marion would be there. Now I wasn't even sure she wanted to be my friend, let alone follow God. "Why don't we go see Pastor Andy? He's a really neat—"

"I don't want anything to do with churches," Marion said, standing and brushing sand from her pants.

"He'd answer your questions."

The wind whipped up and blew Marion's hair. She crumpled her brown bag. "I don't need to talk. I know the answers to my questions. My dad's seeing a doctor in Denver tomorrow. They say it might be his last chance."

CHAPTER 8

Bryce

Mr. Gerrill's house wasn't far from school, and it felt good to ride my bike. After basketball season I didn't exercise much, probably because my legs felt like Jell-O by the last game, and I could feel the muscles starting to work again.

Mrs. Gerrill welcomed me and offered me something to drink. I wanted a Coke, but to be polite I just asked for water. She led me to her husband's shop, and I noticed the smell of wood shavings. I think new-cut wood is one of the best smells on earth.

"Tell me all about your find," Mr. Gerrill said.

As I described the items, a tear came to his eye.

"Is there something wrong?" I said.

"I was just thinking about what those boys went through."

"You know where the wallets came from?"

He opened a drawer and leafed through some files. "I've got a pretty good idea. Before that building was a school, it was owned by the government. There was a bus station in town, and the train came through here too. Soldiers heading west. The main floor was an office, and the upstairs had bedrooms."

"I saw a bunch of ratty old blankets in the boxes we took out of there."

He nodded and pulled out a black-and-white picture. A soldier stood in front of the building. It looked the same, just not as many houses around it.

"My uncle stayed there on his way to California."

"What about the wallets?"

"Probably stolen by someone and jammed into the ceiling. It's a shame because that was most likely all the money those soldiers had."

The more I listened, the madder it made me. To steal is terrible, but to steal from people who want to serve their country is even worse.

"Is it possible to get the wallets back to the owners?" I said.

He rubbed his chin. "The stuff sounds old. A lot of people are probably gone, but if you get me a list, I'll search my database and get you all the addresses I can." He gave me his e-mail address. "That's nice of you to do this."

CHAPTER 9

❀ Ashley ❀

I was so upset about the conversation with Marion that I forgot about the rose card until I was almost home. I circled back and went to my locker as our custodian, Mr. Patterson, passed with a big trash bin.

"Can't get enough of school, huh, Ashley?" He chuckled. I think Mr. Patterson knows every kid's name in our school.

"Left something in my locker," I said.

"Have at it, girl."

It felt like I was carrying around a sackful of rocks, but something about Mr. Patterson's smile and voice took away the weight of the day. Mom can do that too. Leigh usually adds rocks to my pile.

I turned the combination and noticed something weird at the bottom of the locker. Through the vents I saw movement inside. "Mr. Patterson, would you come here a minute?" I called.

He loped along, his keys jangling. I pictured him running after grandkids at a park, smiling from ear to ear. "What can I do for you?"

I pointed. "Something's in there, and I think it might be alive."

He raised his eyebrows. "Alive? Did you plant some magic beans?" That brought another chuckle as he peeked into the holes and lifted the latch.

I stood back and gasped when three heart-shaped balloons came spilling out of the locker. "How did those get in there?"

"Looks like Ashley Timberline has a boyfriend."

I took out the balloons and shoved the card into my backpack. Someone had gone to a lot of trouble to surprise me.

"Anything else I can do, Miss Heartbreaker?"

I shook my head, closed the door, and walked off. He just laughed.

I tried to think who might have put the balloons there. I couldn't come up with any ideas, but a little piece of my heart hoped they were from Duncan Swift.

CHAPTER 10

Bryce

The deadline for entering the writing contest was Friday, and though I'd told Ashley I'd been working on it, I'd hit writer's block. Every time I sat down at the computer, I froze. I had plenty of ideas—everything from retelling what had happened to us at Tres Peaks to a story about a country bumpkin who falls in love with a woman lawyer. I couldn't decide.

Not entering wasn't an option, because the prizes were excellent. I sat at the computer and stared at the screen. Mom was making dinner, and Dylan played with his cars at the coffee table. I told her I couldn't think with all the noise, so instead of moving him (which would have brought on a Dylan war) she let me use her computer.

I grabbed the bag of wallets and headed for her office. She has pictures of writers on her wall as well as things they've said. One quote is by the guy who wrote *Charlotte's Web.* It says, "A writer should concern himself with whatever absorbs his fancy, stirs his heart, and unlimbers his typewriter." I wished I could unlimber the computer keys.

Mom's desk was clear except for a few magazines, so I put the bag down and glanced out the window. A white van was parked across from our driveway. Weird. Nobody parks on that road. When I pushed the curtains back to get a better look, the van pulled away.

I turned Mom's computer on and stared at the blinking cursor. Some athletes have children who become good at sports, and I wondered if writers' kids ever follow in their parents' fingertips. Mom writes as Virginia Caldwell. All the Christian bookstores have her books, and I've even seen them in Wal-Mart.

After a few minutes of staring, I looked through the wallets. All the guys in the pictures looked young, like they had their whole lives ahead of them. I wondered how many had survived the war.

I put the story aside and typed in the names, birthdays, and other data from the licenses, then pasted the info into an e-mail to Mr. Gerrill. As I put them away, I noticed a strange bulge in the wallet of a man named Patrick Elkins. Behind the pictures was a hidden flap. I reached inside and found an unopened letter, perfectly preserved.

I opened the envelope carefully. What I read was amazing and made me think I had my story for the contest.

CHAPTER 11

❀ Ashley ❀

I stashed the balloons in my room and tossed my backpack on the bed. It wasn't long before Dylan ran in and found them. "Who are those from?" he said.

I hesitated, which was my downfall.

"Ashley's got a boyfriend!" Dylan said.

"I don't have a boyfriend," I said, blushing.

Dylan grabbed a balloon and hopped on the bed, bouncing like Tigger after a double latte. "Ash-ley's in love! Ash-ley's in love!" he chanted.

I grabbed his hand, pried the balloon loose, and pulled him into the hall, locking the door behind us. I called for Mom but she didn't answer, so I dragged him outside to the swings.

"Why don't you want anyone to know you have a boyfriend?" he said.

"I don't have a boyfriend. Someone just gave me a few balloons."

"Who?"

I gave him my big-sister sigh. "Dylan, stay right here, okay?"

"Sure."

I ran back inside and unlocked my door, riffled through my backpack until I found the card, and went back outside.

Dylan's swing had slowed to a crawl. "Push me!" he yelled.

I did, then pulled out the card. Around the red rose was a bunch of other fading, drooping flowers. Everything was black-and-white except for the rose. I opened the card, and on the inside were these words in bold letters:

Simply stated, you're one of a kind.

Underneath was a note written in red ink.

Ashley, if you're not going with anyone to the dance, would you go with me? It would be the highlight of my life. If so, tape a red heart to the front of your locker tomorrow.

Sinsearly,
Your Secret Admirer

The whole thing sent a shiver down my spine. Not only because it was so sweet, but because Secret Admirer couldn't spell *sincerely.* Duncan had always had trouble with spelling, so he was still in the running, but if it was him, why didn't he sign his name?

CHAPTER 12

Bryce

In a burst of creativity, I wrote my story, "The Unopened Letter." I made up the name Tom Toomer and said he was headed to war. Just before he left, he got a letter from his girlfriend and stuck it in his wallet. That night someone stole it, and he never got to read it.

I opened the letter and typed most of it word for word, taking out some parts that were too mushy or didn't make sense. Here's what I wrote.

> Tom,
>
> I'm sorry things got heated and angry before you left. I feel bad that the last thing you might remember about me is that

I was crying when you ran to your bus. I didn't mean to hurt your feelings with Dave, but it was innocent, I swear. He asked me out, and I told him I couldn't go. He came to my house, and I sat in his car and told him I couldn't see him anymore, that you and I were getting serious and I didn't want to give him false hopes. That's when you walked up to the car.

I want you to know how much I love you. I know I don't express myself very well. I hide things I feel because I've been hurt so many times, I guess. I've finally realized what you mean to me. I'm sorry it took me so long to answer your proposal. I guess I was scared. But I know now that I want to spend the rest of my life with you.

You are a special guy. The way you make me laugh, your smile, your kindness and gentleness—all of that tells me that you are a quality person. I only hope I wasn't too late. Wouldn't it be fun to show this letter to our grandkids? I pray it will happen.

Tom, if you decide not to give me another chance, if for some reason you don't believe me, I will wait for you. My heart is yours. I can't believe I let you go without telling you how I really feel, but my hope is that you could sense it and this letter will show my feelings are genuine.

Stay safe. I will pray for you every day. Thank you for serving your country and being a true patriot.

All my love,
Victoria

The only thing I changed in the letter was the girl's name. I just couldn't force myself to put Velma at the bottom, so I changed it to Victoria. Sounds more romantic than Velma, I think.

The basic story was that the guy went to war, got hurt, and was lying in a hospital bed next to a dying soldier. The dying guy said he was sorry for the bad things he'd done, and he wanted to confess. Since there wasn't a pastor or priest there, he asked Tom to listen. Tom felt nervous but did it anyway.

The guy told him lots of bad things he'd done in high school, and then he choked up. "And the really rotten thing I did before getting shipped out—I don't think God could ever forgive me."

"What did you do?" Tom said.

"On the night before we left, I stole a bunch of wallets from the guys in my barracks."

Tom sat up. "Where were you?"

Tom gasped when the man told him it was his barracks. "What did you do with the wallets?"

"I took all the money, then hid them. I didn't want to get caught."

"Where did you hide them?" Tom said.

The man thrashed in his bed. "I don't want to die with this on my conscience."

"God will understand. Where did you put them?"

"Why do you want to know?"

"Because one of them was mine, and there was a letter in there I never read. I have a feeling I should have."

"I hid them in a heating vent in the ceiling." The guy fell back on his bed and died.

A few months later, when Tom returned to the U.S., he went back to the barracks, found the hidden wallets, and read the letter from his sweetheart.

He was so excited about her love that he caught the first bus home. He didn't want to call or write; he had to see her face-to-face.

After waiting hours in the bus terminal and an exhausting bus ride, he finally made it to his hometown. He ran through the streets, unable to hold back a huge smile. Two years had passed since he'd left. He'd never written, never called, but after reading the letter, he felt Victoria would be waiting.

He turned onto the familiar street, his feet carrying him like the wind. Victoria's mother was on the porch and gasped when he called her name. The woman pointed to the street as a car drove up.

Dave parked, and Victoria got out of the car, her mouth open. She had on a wedding ring. And there was a baby in the backseat.

Tom held up the letter. "You said you would wait. You said you loved me."

"I didn't hear from you. You didn't even write. What was I supposed to do?"

Tom dropped the letter to the ground and walked away.

CHAPTER 13

❀ Ashley ❀

"What a sad story!" I said after Bryce finished reading it to us that evening.

"Judges love this kind of thing," Bryce said. "Ends with a twist. You think it's going to end one way, and it comes out totally different."

"A little coincidental though," I said.

"What do you mean?"

"That out of all the military hospitals in the world, your main character happened to be in the bed right next to the guy who stole his wallet."

"It could happen," Bryce said.

I could tell the criticism hurt, and I wished I hadn't said anything.

Mom put a hand over her heart. "Oh, I can't imagine what the poor man went through. Going all that way filled with hope and then his heart breaks."

"Sounds like real life," Leigh said, passing through the living room. She hardly spoke to us anymore because she was either at her part-time job or babysitting or going to movies with her boyfriend, Randy.

"It's only a story," Bryce said, his head down. It looked like there was something about the story he didn't want to tell us.

"It's so well written," Mom said, moving her hands. She does that a lot when she talks about stories. "But I'd rather see a happy ending."

"Like what?"

"I don't know. The guy comes back and the girl is blind, but he marries her anyway."

"You call that happy?" Bryce said. Then his eyes sparked. "Hey, what if he gets injured in the war, and she gives him a kidney or something?"

We just sat there watching Dylan play with his cars on the floor. Suddenly he looked up at me, sensing the lull. "Why don't you tell them about your boyfriend?"

Suddenly *I* wanted to change the subject.

Mom raised her eyebrows and smiled.

"Did Skeeter ask you to the dance?" Bryce said, beaming.

Skeeter Messler. I'd forgotten about him. He's not on my team this year so I don't see him much, but Bryce is right. He's had a crush on me for years.

"It's nothing," I said. "Just a dumb old card."

"A mystery man?" Mom said.

"No, it's—"

"I can set up surveillance," Bryce said. "Tell me where you found the card, and I'll snoop around tomorrow."

CHAPTER 14

Bryce

Ashley didn't want me involved, but I couldn't help myself. I was on a mission from the moment I woke up—whether she liked it or not. She rode the bus, and Mom was out the door for a meeting at church, dragging Dylan behind her. I checked Ashley's room and found some balloons but nothing else. You could buy those at any grocery store, so they didn't provide any clues.

Before I left the empty house, I picked up the phone to call Duncan, because I knew Ashley had a thing for him. The handset made a weird noise, so I hung up, picked it up again, and listened to a buzz loud enough to clear wax from my ears. Then I hung up and it suddenly rang. "Hello?"

Nothing on the other end. Just a dial tone. I called Duncan, but he had already left, so I thanked Mrs. Swift and headed for my bike.

When I got outside, a white van pulled away from the road in front of our house and kicked up dust. Was it the same one from before? Maybe Ashley's admirer wanted to deliver something to our house. Or maybe it was Randy delivering something for Leigh.

I was feeling good about my story as I chained my bike at school. I decided to turn it in to Mrs. Ferguson, one of our English teachers. She told me to plug in my thumb drive to her computer and copy it to her contest folder.

I headed back to the hall and watched for anyone holding balloons. I spotted Duncan at the end of the hall. He'd said something mean about Ashley close to Valentine's Day, and I wondered if he'd changed his mind.

I gave him a high five, like we do on the basketball court, and pushed him toward the lockers. "So, what's up with you and my sister?"

He looked confused. "What do you mean?"

I just stared at him.

"Come on, Timberline, what?"

"Just wondered if anything is going on—that's all," I said.

Duncan pushed past me. "You're weird, Timberline."

CHAPTER 15

❋ Ashley ❋

I put my lunch in my locker and hung around until most people had gone to class. I closed it and looked for anyone suspicious. Everybody seemed busy, talking and laughing. There's excitement when we have only a few weeks left of school.

I was about to stick the little red heart on my locker door when I hesitated. Something didn't feel right—I was interested, but I couldn't be sure until I knew the mystery person. I shoved the heart into my pocket and pulled out a packet of sticky notes.

I might be interested, I wrote, *but I don't know who you are. Tell me.* I stuck the note on the locker and folded it.

I was on my way to first period, watching for anyone with a heart-shaped box of chocolates, and I spotted Randy's little brother, Derek. Randy is tall, with muscles and lots of athletic ability. His little brother is short and wears glasses that make him look like a computer geek.

"Derek, how's Randy? We haven't seen him much lately."

He looked at me like I had bean sprouts in my teeth. "Leigh never told you? She dropped him. Like lava."

"What?"

"Yeah, they broke up a couple weeks ago. Randy's been moping around the house like he struck out four times in one game. That sister of yours is brutal."

"Did Randy tell you she dumped him?"

"Not in so many words. I can just tell. He even talked to that youth-pastor guy. He came over to our house."

The hallway was nearly empty so I told Derek to hurry to class. I walked into mine just as the bell rang. Perfectly placed in the middle of my desk was a tiny stuffed puppy holding a red heart. He had a cute smile on his face, and his eyes were hearts.

"Did you see who put this here?" I said to Hayley, who sat right in front of me.

She shrugged and looked away. "It was there when I sat down."

No one had seen who put it there. Underneath the dog was a small folded piece of paper. I unfolded it carefully.

> Ashley, I hope you left the red heart on your locker. I'll be watching.

CHAPTER 16

Bryce

After school, I checked my e-mail. I wondered if Mr. Gerrill had discovered anything about Patrick Elkins. Part of me felt guilty for reading the letter, but if I ever found the guy, I figured he'd understand. But would he understand that I used it in the contest?

I shook the thought off and scrolled through the messages. Nothing from Mr. Gerrill, but I did have junk e-mail trying to sell me insurance and medicine. I deleted those and found one from Duncan.

What was with you today, Timberline? Duncan wrote. *If your sister has a problem, tell her to talk with me.*

I hit the Reply button and stared at the blinking cursor. Was

Duncan the one? *I think you know what I'm talking about.* I shot the message to him.

A message blipped on my screen from Mr. Gerrill. *Bryce, I checked my database of veterans. Of the 12 names you gave me, 3 came up KIA, or killed in action. Sorry, buddy.*

Not half as sorry as their families, I thought.

His message continued. *I'm sending the family members' addresses where you could send the wallets. They may want them for sentimental reasons.*

He listed the addresses and gave others from his database who were certain matches. *The only one I can't track down for sure is Patrick Elkins. I did find a guy in Iowa, but you may want to check before you send his stuff. Thanks for what you're doing.*

CHAPTER 17

❈ Ashley ❈

After the bell, I rode my bike to the high school. The fields were filled with kids running, stretching, and practicing. People swarmed the tennis courts and soccer field.

I parked, headed to the baseball field at the top of the hill, and climbed into the metal stands to watch the guys practice. I spotted Randy right away in center field, his cap pulled low. The batter hit a long fly ball over his head, and Randy turned and sprinted toward the fence. When he reached the dirt track, he looked up, found the ball, and caught it like it was a marshmallow tossed by a kindergartener. He threw it all the way in to the second baseman on the fly.

To my right, a guy in a suit talked on a cell phone, laughing and shaking his head. I wondered if he was somebody's father or maybe a scout from another high school.

When it was Randy's turn to hit, he loped in from the outfield, not even breathing hard when he got to the dugout. He pulled his batting gloves on and picked up three bats before he found the one he wanted. Kind of like Leigh looking for an outfit.

He dug his left foot into the dirt, took a few swings, then eyed his coach on the mound. The crack of the bat surprised me—it sounded like someone breaking a tree limb. The ball cleared the left-field fence by 20 feet.

Everybody on the field stopped and watched it sail. The guy on the phone just stared.

Randy hit the next three pitches hard into left, center, and right, the last one short-hopping the fence.

A few minutes later the coach called everyone in for a pep talk.

When the coach finished, I got Randy's attention and he climbed up to sit with me. His uniform was sweat stained and he had a lot of dirt on his rear, but it didn't seem to bother him. He had a huge wad of bubble gum in his cheek. "To what do I owe this honor?"

I smiled. "I could lie and say I just came to watch."

He nodded and looked at the field. "Leigh told you?"

"Actually, no. I found out another way. Pastor Andy acted strange the other day too."

"He's been a good friend," Randy said.

"What happened?"

"Long story. Hardest thing I've ever had to do, letting go of your sister."

"You dumped *her*?"

"*Dumped* isn't the right word."

"Sorry."

He sighed. "You know I've been attending your church."

"I've seen you a lot."

"Well, I had a long talk with Pastor Andy—several of them. He encouraged me to follow God, to turn my life over to him. He said if I did that, it would be hard to date someone who's so against God."

"What happened when you talked with Leigh?"

"She basically said I had to choose between her and Jesus."

"Sounds like something she would say."

"I've been praying God would change her mind, that she would believe, but I couldn't live a double life."

"Double life?"

"Sneaking off to church. Reading books I know she'd laugh at. I finally told her that God had changed me and I wanted her to know the same forgiveness, but I wasn't going to force her."

"What did she say?"

"Cussed. Said I was a monk going into a monastery."

That sounded like her too, but I didn't say it. Leigh can be really mean, even to people she likes. "So you finally did it, huh?"

Randy smiled. "Yeah, and God's been working on me so long it was natural. No bells or angels clapping. I just felt like no matter what happens, I'm on his side now. I just wish . . ." He took off his cap and looked down. His hair was wet, and beads of sweat ran down his face. When he looked at me, his eyes were red. "I like Leigh a lot, and I honestly want the best for her. I can't imagine her running from God her whole life."

I nodded and took a deep breath. "I feel the same way. About Sam too. I almost think they already believe; they're just being stubborn about it. But we can't twist their arms. It's up to them."

Randy nodded. "That's what Pastor Andy said, but I wish there was something more I could do."

"Pray," I said. "We've been doing it for years. I even ordered a DVD with one of Leigh's favorite actresses who became a Christian. She talks about her faith and why she thinks God is real."

"What did Leigh say about it?" Randy said.

"Took one look and called the actress a loser. Wouldn't even pop it in the player."

The man with the cell phone walked up behind Randy. I nodded toward him and Randy turned.

"I don't mean to interrupt," the man said. "I'm Nelson Maloney. From Boston."

Randy jumped to his feet and wiped his hand on his uniform. "Mr. Maloney, it's good to meet you."

Nelson smiled. "You got my letter."

"Yes, sir. I've been hoping you'd show up at one of my games."

"Oh, I have. Last week against Widefield. Three homers and a walk. Threw a guy out at the plate."

Randy stifled a grin. "That was a good game to see."

"Can we talk?" he said, motioning toward the parking lot.

Randy looked at me with eyes as big as the numbers on the centerfield scoreboard.

"You have to tell me about this later," I said.

Randy just grinned.

CHAPTER 18

Bryce

Mom gave me bubble mailers so I could send the wallets. I addressed them all and printed a note to send with each.

I was looking at the Patrick Elkins information when a message popped up on the computer. That was strange because Sam had installed a program that zapped every pop-up.

Liberty Antivirus has detected an infection in your system. An unknown Trojan, virus, or outside party may be attempting to access vital information about you or your computer. We suggest you run Spyzinger now to eliminate any threat.

I called Mom over, and she said to run the program. The computer just stared at us, and I finally rebooted it.

That's when Ashley ran into the kitchen. "You'll never believe it!" she shouted. "Never in a million years!"

"You're marrying Skeeter Messler?" I said.

She sneered, then brightened. "It's about Randy!"

"You're marrying Randy?" I said.

"Bryce," Mom said. "What is it, honey?"

Ashley told us about the guy from Boston. I knew he had to be from the Red Sox. "When I rode away, the guy was handing Randy some papers. You think it could be a contract?"

"They'll probably send him to the minors or the instructional league first," I said. "Unless Randy has already committed to a college."

"He hasn't," Leigh said. She was at the stairs, staring at Ashley.

"Isn't it great?" Ashley said. "Maybe someday we'll see him on TV playing center field."

"Maybe he'll get lucky and get traded to the Cubs," I said.

"You call that luck?" Leigh said, not taking her eyes off Ashley. "What were you doing over there?"

"I didn't know I needed your permission," Ashley said. I could tell that had slipped out because Ashley immediately winced.

Leigh looked mad, balling her fists, her face red. If she'd been a little teapot short and stout, you wouldn't have wanted to touch her handle or her spout.

Just then the phone rang, and even though I like watching fireworks, I grabbed it.

"How's everything going there?" Sam said.

"Just great. Ashley heard the Red Sox are interested in Randy."

"Doesn't surprise me," Sam said in his drawly voice.

I told him about the computer problem, and he seemed concerned. He asked me to go through a series of prompts, navigating my way through the computer. Sam took me to places I didn't know existed.

"Sounds like somebody's hacked into our network," he said. "Shut the thing down and have your mother unplug her modem upstairs."

I wanted to tell him about the guy I was trying to locate, but Mom motioned for the phone.

CHAPTER 19

❀ Ashley ❀

I followed Leigh upstairs and knocked lightly on her door. "Leigh?"

"Go away."

"I didn't mean to be nosy."

"Go away."

"I just wanted to find out what was wrong."

"Go away."

"Randy told me some stuff about how he feels toward you."

Silence.

"I thought you'd want to hear it."

I heard her bed creak, footsteps, then the door unlocking. When I heard the bed creak again, I walked inside.

"What did he say?" she said, her face muffled in a pillow.

I sat on the bed. "Randy told me breaking up was the hardest thing he's ever done. I could tell by his eyes that he wasn't lying."

"Bet you're glad he's gotten religious on me. Going to heaven and all that."

"I'm glad he believes in God, but I'm sad you're not together." I leaned closer. "He told me he wants the best for you. That he hopes you'll find—"

"He wants me to find God and raise my hands and read the Bible and . . ." She was on the verge of tears. "You talk about God loving you, but I think he hates me."

"Why would you say that?"

"Because he figures out how to take away everything I love!"

CHAPTER 20

Bryce

Mom went to her bedroom to talk with Sam. Dylan banged on her door, and I asked what he wanted.

"She didn't hug me when I came home from school."

"Let her talk and when she comes out she'll hug you."

"But I want one now."

I picked him up and squeezed him until he turned red. He squealed and chased me outside to the swings. Frodo barked at Pippin and tried to wrestle with him, but Pippin just sat there. He's older and getting slower.

When Mom came back to the kitchen, I ran inside and asked what Sam said.

Her face turned grim. "He's back into it again."

"Into what?"

"The terrorist thing. He's working on some special case."

"What case?"

"I can't say much, but it might have something to do with the man who shot down your father's plane."

"Asim bin Asawe?"

"What about him?" Ashley said, walking into the room. "I thought they'd caught him . . . or he was dead."

"Well, apparently not, because there's been some chatter on the Internet about something big happening in the U.S. soon."

"An attack?" I said.

She nodded, staring out the window at Dylan. Suddenly she turned to us. "You remember how important it is not to—"

"We know how to keep it quiet," I said.

She smiled. "Yeah, I guess you do."

"Any idea what the terrorists are planning?" Ashley said.

Mom bit her lip. "I'm going to tell you this because you asked, but you have to promise me—"

"Mom, we're not going to tell anyone," Ashley said.

She smoothed the tablecloth. "Sam said the networks they've tapped into are calling it Operation Hammer or something like that."

"Hammer?" I said. "Like someone's going to smash us?"

"Maybe it's a nuclear bomb," Ashley said.

"They don't know what it means, but it sounds bad," Mom said.

I racked my brain, trying to think of any special dates the terrorists might want to use to stage an attack. "Maybe they're going to attack Home Depot stores and steal hammers."

It didn't lighten the room.

"Did they spell it h-a-m-m-e-r?" Ashley said.

"Sam said it was h-a-m-a-r."

"Hamar," I said. "Sounds like some biblical name, doesn't it?"

"You're thinking of Tamar," Ashley said. "We just heard about her in Sunday school this past week."

"Oh yeah, the lady who—"

"Let's not talk about that story," Mom said.

It was an ugly story, but Pastor Andy had applied it to our lives.

The three of us just stood there, trying to think of what a hammer or hamar had to do with the United States.

"Maybe it's the name of one of the terrorists," Ashley said.

"Or hamburger without the 'burg.'"

I walked into the living room and stared at the dark computer. I wanted to find out more about my veteran in Iowa or look up *hamar.*

Just then Dylan burst through the kitchen door and jumped into Mom's arms. He finally got his hug.

CHAPTER 21

❀ Ashley ❀

Randy pulled into our driveway. Dylan ran out and wouldn't stop hugging him. He does that to people he really likes.

Randy didn't come any closer than the front porch, but I could tell he was excited. "I promised to tell you—that guy is a Red Sox scout who goes to high schools. My coach recommended me."

"Did you sign anything?" Bryce said.

"Not yet. My dad wants to talk with someone who understands contracts." He held out the papers to my mom. "We thought you might help."

"Me?" Mom chuckled. "I've seen a lot of book contracts, but . . . well, let me take a look." She took the pages inside to copy.

Randy told us more. "They want me to play this summer in an instructional league, maybe play winter ball in Mexico. If I do okay, I'll play single A or double A next year."

"That means you won't go to college?" I said.

"Right. I'll give this a try and maybe go to the big leagues. If I don't make it, I can go to school."

Mom came back, flipping through the pages. "That's a hefty signing bonus. I assume you keep that money no matter what happens."

"That's what Mr. Maloney said. He's talking to my dad now. Did the contract look legit?"

Mom nodded. "Sure did, but I don't trust my knowledge. I'd like to send it to a friend who's a lawyer. He'll be able to tell us for sure."

"I'd appreciate that, Mrs. Timberline."

"I'll have him call you after he looks it over."

Randy stepped back, looked up, and removed his hat. "Hey."

"Hey," Leigh said from the window. "Exciting stuff, huh?"

"Yeah. Maybe I'll catch a fly ball in front of the Green Monster."

"Probably hit a few over the Green Monster too."

Randy kicked the dirt and put his hat on. I saw a glint of a tear in one eye. He headed for his truck, then turned to me. "Almost forgot. I found this in your paper box. It's for you."

I took the card. *Ashley* was written on the front in red ink.

"He strikes again," Bryce said.

I stuffed the card in my pocket and went back inside.

CHAPTER 22

Bryce

Even though it was getting dark, Mom said I could go to the library. Randy dropped me off at a building the size of a small house, which it used to be. They have computers along one wall where you can search for books or hook up to the Internet.

I pulled up a phone-number search site and typed in *Patrick Elkins* in Iowa. I got five listings, and only one matched the age I was looking for. I wrote down the number. Before I exited, I typed in Velma's name in Idaho. I had her address from the letter. A number popped up, and I wrote it down.

As I walked home, I had a lot on my mind. Sam working in

Washington. Ashley's secret admirer. A possible summer job at the Toot Toot Café. Starting high school next year. And Lynette Jarvis. How could I not think about the prettiest girl in school, even if she hates my guts?

At the top of the list was Velma's letter. What if someone at the contest found out I'd copied it?

Eighth-grade graduation was also on my mind. I knew Mom would be there and Sam, if he was in town, but nothing can replace your own dad. Every trophy, report card, holiday, and birthday just put more distance between my real dad and me. Lately I'd had dreams of Dad coming into my room, sitting on my bed, and talking. They felt real.

By the time I made it home it was dark. I grabbed the phone and dialed the Iowa number.

"Hello?" an older man said.

"Mr. Elkins?"

"Yes."

"My name is Bryce. I'm calling from Colorado."

"You're not selling something, are you? Because this number is on the do-not-call list—"

"I'm not selling anything, sir. I think I have something of yours."

"What's that?"

"Were you in the military?"

"Sure was. Infantry."

"Did you spend any time in Colorado?"

He paused. "Come to think of it, I did. Train broke down in some little backwater town out there. Had to wait a couple of days."

I wiped sweat from my hands. "Did you lose a wallet?"

He didn't answer for a long time. "A wallet? No, I don't think I did."

"Does the name Velma Coleman mean anything to you?"

I had to repeat the name until he heard it correctly. Then he said, "I knew a Rhonda Coleman. You talking about her?"

I explained that I'd found a wallet with Velma's letter to him in it. I also read his Social Security number to him.

"Son, I'm afraid you've got the wrong man. That's not my number."

CHAPTER 23

❀ Ashley ❀

After Randy and Bryce left, I ran to my room and locked the door. I closed the blinds, turned off the light, and lay down slowly on the comforter. I lit my favorite candle and watched it flicker in my dresser mirror. Maybe I've seen too many movies, but the whole room felt romantic.

I sniffed the envelope. It had a familiar, musty smell. Not perfume or aftershave—it was different. I opened it carefully, pulled out the card, and stared at a picture of a little boy dressed in a suit and hat, his tie askew, holding a flower arrangement behind his back. He was leaning over a tricycle, about to kiss a little girl in a polka-dot dress.

My heart fluttered. It suddenly felt warm in the room. I giggled. *Who* is *this guy?*

The card read, *Flowers and candy are inexpensive. It's a lot harder to give your heart away. You have mine.*

I let the card fall to my chest. Then I pulled my pillow over my face, kicked my legs, and laughed like a hyena.

Knock-knock.

"Who is it?" I said.

"It's Mom. Are you all right?"

"I'm fine."

"I thought I heard you crying."

"No, I'm fine."

"Okay," she said, but it didn't sound like she meant it.

I opened the card to the note on the inside cover.

Dear Ashley,

I saw the note on your locker. I guess it's not fair that you don't know who I am. That's funny because you've known me a long time. We've had troubles, but I hope that's going to change.

I've watched you and have seen how kind you are. Even to people who don't deserve it—like Boo Heckler. I know you and your brother helped him get out of juvie.

You have a lot of courage. Someone told me you saved a dog's life and helped a baby alpaca get born.

You're the prettiest girl in school. One day you'll be in the movies because that's how pretty you are.

I'd better stop or you're going to figure this out. I'm sorry if anything I said or did hurt you. I hope you can forgive me and give me another chance. It would be the highlight of my life.

Sinserely,
Your S. A.

CHAPTER 24

Bryce

In baseball, once you get a strike, you want to swing again. I'd swung and missed with Mr. Elkins, so the next pitch was Velma Coleman. Maybe she would have information. The phone rang a couple of times before an older woman picked up.

"Mrs. Coleman?" I said.

"*Miss* Coleman, yes?"

"Miss Velma Coleman?"

She giggled like a young girl. "Yes. What's this about, son? I've already bought my Boy Scout popcorn for the year."

"I'm not selling anything, ma'am. I'm calling from Colorado about someone you know . . . or used to know."

"Colorado? Well, now you have my interest. Go ahead."

"Does the name Patrick Elkins mean anything to you?"

She paused, and then her voice turned serious. "Yes, it does. It means a great deal to me. Why do you ask?"

I told her about the house I helped clean, and I could tell she was getting impatient. "I found an old wallet of his—something he had years ago."

"What does this have to do with me?" she said, sounding frail.

"I found your letter in that wallet. I think the wallet was stolen—there was no money inside, but your letter was tucked inside, unopened."

"Pat never read my letter . . . ," she said, thinking it through.

"Miss Coleman," I said after a few moments, "do you know anything about him? Did he ever come back to town?"

"He did." She sounded short of breath. "But I never . . ."

"You never what?"

"I never spoke with him. I assumed he had read the letter and didn't want to forgive me." A chair squeaked, and it sounded like she sat. "Did you open it? Did you read it?"

I can't lie to old ladies. "Yes. I was curious."

"It's okay. I'm glad you did. Otherwise you wouldn't have called me."

"I tried to find Mr. Elkins, but I came up empty. Do you know if he's still alive?"

"I lost track. . . . I put him out of my mind as much as I could."

"Did you ever marry anyone?"

She laughed. "Are you proposing? No, I never married. Had a few proposals of sorts, but I decided to throw myself into my profession."

"Which was?"

"Teaching. I taught at the elementary school for 30 years. I still volunteer at the library and do story time for the little ones. I guess you could say the children became the love of my life."

"Did Mr. Elkins ever marry?" I said.

She paused. "He still has family in this area. I heard through the grapevine that he had gotten married and moved down south."

CHAPTER 25

❀ Ashley ❀

I woke up smiling the next morning. I had dreamed I was a princess going to a ball, and the prince looked like Duncan.

"You're chipper this morning," Mom said as I floated to breakfast. "Who was the card from?"

"Who told you about the card?"

"Your brother."

I dug into my cereal and waved at Bryce as he left for school. I didn't feel like riding my bike all that way when I just wanted to think. The bus came, and I sat behind Marion Quidley. She gave me a half wave, staring at a magazine.

My thoughts were on the card (hidden in the top drawer of my dresser) and who might have sent it. I hoped it wasn't Skeeter Messler—but even if it was him, it was nice for someone to think of me as pretty.

The sky seemed a little bluer. A flock of geese hung in the air, flapping their wings. Kids on the bus laughed.

Marion turned and said something over the din. I only made out the word *Duncan.*

"What was that?" I said.

"I said, what was Duncan Swift doing out near your house yesterday?"

"I don't know. Where'd you see him?"

"I was riding with my mom and saw him on his bike. He was alone on your road."

I sat back and smiled.

CHAPTER 26

Bryce

I went outside to eat lunch. Kids were playing touch football in the field, and others were walking around the climbing wall and talking. I noticed a white van parked across the street from the school, and it looked like the one I'd seen near our house. I moved up the hill, but when I got to the top, the driver pulled away. He had on a white painter's hat, and there was a colorful sign on the side door.

Why am I so jumpy these days? I thought.

When I'd finished my lunch, I called Mr. Gerrill and told him what I'd found out about Mr. Elkins.

He didn't seem surprised. "A lot of veterans fall through the cracks, and we don't know where they wind up."

"Any chance of finding him?" I said.

"Not with my current database," he said. "Sorry, Bryce."

I hung up and thought of my options. Miss Coleman had mentioned that Patrick's family members lived in her town. Maybe they could help.

I ran to the computer in the office. I'm an aide to Mr. Gminski, so I get to use the computer for different projects. I logged on and typed in *Elkins* and Miss Coleman's town. A list of four names came up, and I printed them.

Before I logged off, I thought about what Mom had said about Operation Hamar. I typed *hamar* into a search engine. It came up as a town in Norway, an Ethiopian tribe, and a musician's last name. I couldn't find anything even remotely linked to terrorists.

The bell rang, and someone put a hand on my shoulder. "Shouldn't we be getting to class, Mr. Timberline?" Mr. Bookman said.

I hate it when grown-ups use "we" when they're talking about you. I just nodded and grabbed my stuff.

CHAPTER 27

❀ Ashley ❀

I didn't have any classes with Duncan during the morning, but I hoped to see him at lunch. I ran to my locker (where there were no new messages) and then hustled into the lunchroom.

Duncan was a creature of habit. Like baseball players who wear the same T-shirt for good luck, Duncan always sits in the same seat. I situated myself across from his table at a spot where chess-club types gather.

Duncan entered like a king, swaggering from battle. He got his lunch tray and went through the line, opening his milk without spilling a drop. He glided to the table like an ice-skater. Just watching him walk gave me goose bumps.

"What are you doing here?" someone said behind me.

I turned to see Skeeter Messler and the rest of the chess team gawking at me like I was Snow White.

"Is this your table?" I said innocently. "There's plenty of room."

The guys shrugged in better unison than our band and took their seats.

I looked back at Duncan, but he was talking and laughing with his friends.

"You going to the dance?" Skeeter said.

I glanced at him, and a look of hope spread on his face. "I'm not sure," I said.

"Has anybody asked you?" He was eating a baloney sandwich, and some of the white bread stuck to his front teeth.

"Sort of, but not really. . . ." I couldn't believe I almost gave up my secret to the nerdiest guy in school.

"Which is it?" another chess guy said. "You're either invited or you aren't."

I looked over and noticed Duncan staring at our table. I waved, but he was evidently looking at Skeeter.

"Skeeter wants to ask you something," someone said.

"Guys, I think I should be going—"

"No, wait," Skeeter said. "If you're not sure, would you go to the dance with *me*?" He looked like a frightened pup about to be trampled by a Clydesdale.

I opened my mouth, then looked at Duncan and remembered how much his words had hurt me. "Let's talk over there—in private."

It was a long walk to the stairs, but it gave me time to think. It made it harder when I turned to Skeeter and saw the frightened puppy had turned into an excited puppy. He did everything but wag his tail and chew on my shoelace.

"What do you think?" he said. "My mom said she'd spring for a limo."

"You've talked to your parents about this?"

"Just my mom," he said.

"Listen, Skeeter, that sounds like fun, but the truth is . . ."

Duncan stood and threw his stuff into the trash.

"The truth is what?" Skeeter said.

"I don't even know if I want to go."

"But aren't you on the student council?"

"Yeah, but—"

"I get it. It's a religious thing."

"Not really. Some church kids have rules against that kind of thing but not my mom and dad."

"So why won't you go with me?"

I crossed my arms and sighed. "Skeeter, I like you but not as a boyfriend."

"You don't have to be my girlfriend. You don't even have to dance with me. It would just be, you know . . . the highlight of my life."

I stared at him. The words seemed familiar. Then it came to me. The last words on the cards. "Skeeter, are you the one?"

"The one what?"

"Who's been putting stuff on my locker? leaving cards at my house? calling yourself my secret admirer?"

He snarled, "I'm desperate but not *that* desperate. Someone's stalking you?"

I poked a finger in his face. "Promise you won't tell *anybody,* understand?"

He thought a minute. "If I promise, will you go to the dance with me?"

I turned and walked away.

CHAPTER 28

Bryce

In English class, Mrs. Ferguson asked if anyone wanted to read their composition. We all looked at each other, wondering if anyone would bite.

Chuck Burly finally raised a hand and said he had entered the screenplay competition. He told us the story of an overweight college football player named Bubba who always played defense. Bruised and battered after every game, he dreamed about playing offense.

"When his mother asks him to get some potatoes from the basement, he finds an old lamp, and a genie offers him three wishes.

Bubba can't believe it and asks for a triple cheeseburger with everything. It appears in his hands. He gets so excited he uses his second wish for a supersize ice-cream sundae."

By now, the whole class was riveted.

"Bubba realizes he has only one wish left, and he can't decide. His family is poor, so they could use money, but he goes with the wish of being on offense. The next night, after a running back gets hurt, Bubba pesters the coach and the man puts him in. When the quarterback fakes a handoff to him, Bubba grabs the ball and runs for a touchdown."

The story got more interesting, teams wanting Bubba to jump to the pros, his family seeing him as a human lottery ticket, and the whole thing ending with Bubba losing his powers and just being a mediocre guy on defense.

"The moral is just be who you are instead of someone else and you'll find your place in the world," Chuck said.

Not bad, I thought.

A couple others read their stories.

Then Lynette Jarvis stood. "I actually wrote a poem."

Mrs. Ferguson nodded, and Lynette took a deep breath. I couldn't help but take one myself because of the way her hair shone in the fluorescent light.

She looked up—straight at me. "My poem is called 'Being Forgiven.'"

It hangs like a weight around my neck
The things I've done, the things I've said.
Exposed, my plan buried me instead of him,
And now shame floods and surrounds, pulling me lower.
They call it gravity, but it feels like guilt.

I dream I am somewhere else, and no one knows
The things I've done, the things I've said.
But when I open my eyes, I'm still here in my bed,
In the town where no one knows, but everyone should.
In the town where I'm stalked like a lion.

Just when I think the death sentence is coming,
When my life is about to end,
He speaks.
He takes the weight.
Removes the chain.
Lifts it with words.
And I am light again.
Alive.
Forgiven.

When she finished, she looked up from the page. Everybody in the room clapped but me, because I was stunned to see her smiling at me.

CHAPTER 29

❀ Ashley ❀

I knew I'd find Duncan outside after school, so I grabbed my stuff after the bell. I noticed a folded piece of paper at the bottom of my locker. Red ink.

> Ashley,
>
> I saw you in the lunchroom with Skeeter. Did you think he's your secret admirer? I'm hurt. I thought you'd figure out who I am by now.
>
> I'll try to talk with you this weekend. I hope you'll be home Saturday night. Talk to you then.
>
> S. A.

I shoved the note in my backpack and ran. I had to see Duncan *NOW!*

Kids scurried like bees in the hallway, then swarmed toward the buses. Duncan unchained his bike, and Bryce was right next to him.

"Wait up!" I yelled.

Duncan looked at me, then got on his bike. I guess he thought I was calling Bryce.

"Duncan, wait!" I shouted.

He stopped. "What?"

I glanced at Bryce. "It's not polite to stare."

He snickered, shook his head, and rode away.

"I want you to know that I'm flattered by what you've been doing," I said.

Duncan gave me a half smile, half frown. "Flattered by what? I don't get it."

"The notes you've been sending."

"Notes?"

"On my locker. *In* my locker. Then at my house."

"Ashley, I don't know what you're talking about."

He'd been caught red-handed. I felt I had to help him. "You don't have to be embarrassed. I've really enjoyed the game of trying to figure it out. The truth is, I was hoping it would be you. I've felt the same way, but I didn't have the courage to tell you." I looked up and met Duncan's eyes. "I'd be glad to go to the dance with you."

Duncan acted like a gnat had flown into his ear and was building a condo behind one eye. "Ashley, I didn't write any notes to you. Honest, I don't know—"

"What were you doing riding your bike by our place? Do you deny that?"

"No, I was on your road because it shortcuts the ride to Hayley's."

"Hayley?" I said.

"Yeah, yesterday I asked her to go to the dance with me."

My jaw dropped, and a 50-pound weight pulled my heart to my stomach.

My backpack was open, and Duncan grabbed the note and scanned it. Then he did something I'll never forget as long as I live. His face showed pity, as if he were looking at a wounded animal he was going to have to shoot. "Ashley, I don't even have a red pen."

I took the page back and stuffed it in my backpack.

"Ashley, I'm sorry. I didn't know . . ."

I waved a hand and turned. "No, I'm sorry." Then my feet were running, kicking up dust. I didn't know which way to run, and it didn't matter because I couldn't see anything.

CHAPTER 30

Bryce

As soon as I got home, I called the first Elkins. The woman on the other end sounded weird, so I tried another. It was a distant cousin of Patrick's.

"Try his brother, Dennis," she said.

He was the third name on my list, so I called. It rang and rang, and no answering machine picked up.

It was almost four o'clock when Ashley walked in the door. Her eyes were a little red, and I wondered if it had anything to do with Duncan.

"Want to ride to the Morrises'?" I said.

She walked past me, then turned. "Yeah, sure."

We have headsets in our helmets so we can talk to each other, but Ashley didn't say a word. I didn't press her and figured she'd talk when she wanted to.

Our alpaca, Amazing Grace, lives on the Morris farm, and she's really grown. She's almost 100 pounds, and Mr. Morris said she can start a family at the end of the summer. A baby alpaca can sell for thousands of dollars, so it makes scooping her poop worth it. Sam says her babies could give us a "full alpaca scholarship" to college.

Since Ashley wasn't talking, I thought about Lynette's poem. I didn't think she'd become a Christian, but it did sound like she'd been blown away that I hadn't tried to get back at her.

One of our pastors says some people need to trust Christians before they can trust God, and that makes sense to me. When some people hear the word *God,* they think about religious people who've done something bad to them. I hoped my forgiving Lynette would cause her to open up a little more to spiritual stuff.

We cleaned Amazing Grace's stall. Alpacas are like cats—they pick a spot and go there all the time.

Mr. Morris came to the barn and thanked us. One of his boys was sick so he couldn't stay long.

A few minutes later I finally got the chance to ask Ashley what was wrong. She kept finding things to do or look at, and it was driving me crazy.

"Ashley, spill it," I said. "You think I'll tell somebody?"

She started crying, and her tears turned to sniffles. I told her a joke, but that didn't help. She grabbed a paper towel from a dispenser and blew her nose. That scared Grace and it made me laugh, which made Ashley smile.

I knew that was the turning point.

CHAPTER 31

❀ Ashley ❀

Bryce already knew a lot about the notes, but he didn't know the whole story. It wasn't until it all tumbled out that I realized how much holding it inside hurt. He listened and didn't make jokes or even smile until I told him I'd ruled out Duncan and Skeeter.

"Sorry," he said. "Just thinking about Skeeter writing *anybody* a love note is funny."

I punched him on the arm, but he didn't hit me back.

He actually patted me on the shoulder. "I heard about Duncan asking Hayley and wanted to tell you, but there was no time."

"I'm okay," I said.

"Yeah, well, Duncan can be a real dodo."

"So can Lynette," I said.

He gave me a strange look, then went into the "thinker's" position—an elbow on one knee, his face scrunched against his fist. "What if this turns out to be some high schooler? What if it's Randy? He gave you one note."

"No way," I said. "How would he have gotten into our school?"

"Derek?"

"I don't think so."

He pursed his lips. "What if it's a teacher? Or Mr. Bookman—he's single."

That made me laugh. "Bryce, it's definitely someone we know. I just don't know who."

"Have you checked your e-mail?" he said.

"Not since Sam said to turn off the computer."

"We can turn it on just for a little while."

Bryce and I talked about all kinds of stuff on the way home. Eighth grade had been a pain, mostly because of our friends. "Why do you think they treated us this way?" I said.

"Because they're all flaky, just like we are. Besides, you know what Mom says about middle school—if we can survive this, we can survive anything."

Bryce turned on the computer, and I logged onto my e-mail fast. Of all the messages, one stood out. In the subject line it said *S. A. to Ashley.* The return address was some weird Yahoo! address that was a bunch of letters and numbers thrown together.

"Where would this guy have gotten my address?" I said.

Bryce leaned forward. "Read it out loud."

"Ashley, I don't know if you saw my note in your locker, so I thought I'd try here. If you're wondering where I got your e-mail address, it was listed in the student council directory."

"That explains it," Bryce said. "Everybody got that handout."

"I'm going to call you tomorrow night," the e-mail continued, *"unless you don't want me to. If it gives you the creeps, I'll stop."*

That part made me feel good. If I could say stop, I was in control.

"Write back, or I'll just talk to you tomorrow evening."

"What do you think?" Bryce said.

I typed a short message back. "Won't hurt to take a call."

Bryce turned the computer off and unplugged it. "I'm glad we have caller ID."

CHAPTER 32

Bryce

Sam still wasn't home by Saturday morning, and I was worried. Last year he'd told us about his life in counterterrorism before Mom met him. It was scary thinking of him going back to it.

Sam had asked me to mow the yard. I kept putting it off, eating more cereal, reading the sports section of the newspaper. The Cubs were on FOX later, and I planned my day around it.

Dylan wandered to the breakfast table, groggy and trailing his Mask Man blanket. "I want breakfast," he said as I stared at the paper. "I know what I want." He poked me on the shoulder. "I know what I want," he repeated.

"World peace?" I said.

He squinted. "No, Apple Jacks."

I got him his bowl and his favorite spoon. He sat on a wobbly stool by the counter and a little aquarium Mom bought for him. I told him he had to eat at the table because he always spills over there.

"Aw, man, I was gonna sit by my fish," he said.

I finished mowing just in time to clean up and watch the Cubs, but Mom said Mrs. Watson called and asked if I would mow her lawn too. I couldn't believe I was missing a nationally televised game.

Mrs. Watson and Mom talked on the porch while I mowed. Peanuts, her Chihuahua, hopped and barked at the front door. When I moved to the back, he ran out his doggy door and barked from the back porch.

I used the string trimmer on her sidewalk and around the fence. When I finished, Mrs. Watson had a fresh glass of lemonade ready. "Go on into the living room," she said.

"But my socks are all grassy and—"

"Well, take them off and wash your legs with the hose." She cackled.

I did and was surprised to see the Cubs on TV inside. They had a big lead by the sixth when Mom got a call from Ashley saying Dylan was up from his nap.

"You'll come back in a couple of weeks and do that again, won't you?" Mrs. Watson said to me, squeezing a $10 bill into my hand before I could leave.

"You don't have to pay for—"

"Just shut your tater trap, young man," she said. "You come back in two weeks or I'll hunt you down."

I laughed at the thought of her hunting anything and waved. Mrs.

Watson had become one of our true friends. I wondered if she ever thought of reentering eighth grade. Ashley and I could use her.

We hadn't even gotten the mower out of the trunk of the car when Ashley called for Mom. Sam was on the phone again. I followed her inside and tried to listen, but she kept saying, "Oh, dear" and stuff like that.

Dylan sat at the table eating a Pop-Tart—the purple kind with the stripes. He had red circles on his forehead that looked like he was infected with something. I knew he had slept on Mom's weird pillows with the plastic things on them.

"You get that injury on the football field?" I said, leaning down.

He opened his mouth and showed me a purple tongue. It was so disgusting that I had to laugh. He chased me into the living room, and Ashley shushed us and turned up the TV. It was a news report about the president raising the terror-alert status.

Mom walked in and stared at the screen.

"What's wrong?" Ashley said.

She tried to smile. "Sam's not sure when he'll be back. Some new developments. They're calling it a major threat."

"What's the target?" I said. "An airliner? A city?"

"This stays here," she said.

"We know," Bryce and I said in unison.

"They're calling it a multiple strike—different locations around the country."

"You mean buses or trains, that kind of thing?" Ashley said.

"They don't know. Sam's analyzing the data."

"They find out what *hamar* means?" I said.

Mom shook her head.

CHAPTER 33

Ashley

I spent the afternoon in my room pacing, scanning my yearbook for secret-admirer candidates. There were a few cute guys and a bunch on my no list.

The phone rang at 6:00, but it was someone from church for Mom. Bryce stayed downstairs, watching caller ID like a hawk. At 7:15 the phone rang again.

I grabbed it and punched the On button. "Hello?"

"Ashley?" a male voice said.

"Yeah, it's me."

"I told you I'd call. Here I am."

My heart flapped like a hummingbird's wings. I sat on the bed and tried to concentrate. "Who *are* you?"

"A secret admirer is supposed to stay a secret."

"Yeah, but if you want to go to the dance, you'll have to tell me. Unless you want to wear a mask the whole time."

Someone ran upstairs fast. Bryce burst in holding a piece of paper.

"If you say you'll go to the dance with me, I'll tell you everything," the guy said.

I grabbed the paper and read: *Pay phone in town. Keep him on the line.*

I gave Bryce the thumbs-up, and he bolted out the door.

"That's not fair," I said into the phone. "You know all about me, but I know nothing about you."

"Not true. You know plenty about me."

"Like what?" I said.

"Ask me a question."

"Okay, do you go to my school?"

He chuckled. It sounded familiar, but I couldn't place it. "Yeah, I go to your school."

"Are you in eighth grade?"

"Right again."

Bryce's ATV zoomed through our yard, and I looked out the window as he headed for town. "Are you on my team?"

"Hey, no fair trying to narrow it down like that," he said. I could tell he was trying to disguise his voice. It was kind of muffled so maybe he had a hand over the receiver. I heard traffic in the background. There are only three pay phones in town. One is near the grocery store. Another is near the 7-Eleven. A third is in the parking lot of a small shopping center.

"All right," I said. "We can just talk if you want."

"Good. How's your family?"

"I guess we're okay. My stepdad's been away so my mom is on edge."

"Any idea when he's coming back?"

"No. He's tied up with work."

"What's he do?"

"I thought I was supposed to ask the questions."

A train whistle sounded in the background.

"Hang on—there's a train going by," he said.

I ran downstairs with the phone and found Mom's cell phone. I dialed Bryce with one hand while I held the home phone with the other. Bryce didn't answer.

"You still there?" Secret Admirer said.

"Yeah, it's just kind of hard to hear you."

"Okay, just another minute," he said.

I text messaged Bryce and marked it urgent so his phone would vibrate. *Secret Admirer near train tracks.*

"Okay, it's gone now," he said.

"Have you lived here all your life?" I said, trying to catch my breath.

"Most people around here have moved from somewhere else, so that's too big a clue. I'll tell you who I am if you'll just go to the dance, Ashley."

I liked it when he said my name. Different faces flashed through my mind, and I wondered if it might be Duncan after all. Maybe he and Hayley had a fight.

When I didn't answer right away, he said, "Guess I'd better be going."

The phone beeped. "No, wait. I have another call coming in. Stay right there."

I pushed the Flash button and answered.

It was Bryce. "Just got your message. I'm on foot. Is he still on the phone?"

"He was till you called. I'll try to keep him on."

I pushed the Flash button again. "You still there?"

"Yeah, and as much as I'm enjoying talking, I think it's time. You'll be hearing from me again soon, Ashley."

"Wait, I have one more question."

The train whistle sounded in the distance and a car passed, but my secret admirer was gone.

Seconds later the call waiting beeped, and it was Bryce, out of breath.

"Did you see him?" I said.

"The phone is just hanging here. He must have seen me coming."

"There's nobody there?"

"Not a soul. There was a weird van I've been seeing around town lately but nobody on foot. We missed him."

PART 2

CHAPTER 34

Dark Man slammed his fist down, shaking the Styrofoam coffee cups on the table. A woman in the corner jumped. "We will go when I say—do you understand?" he spat.

Another man wearing a painter's outfit scooted closer. He had a higher-pitched voice. "You know we respect you, but the longer we wait, the greater the chance of our being detected."

"Do you know how long I've waited to make this man suffer?"

"We do, but this operation is bigger than one man's vengeance. We will bring this country to its knees." The younger man saw the fire in the older man's eyes. At first he thought he would be shot.

But Dark Man put his gun on the table. "You are wise beyond

your years. Operation Hamar is bigger than my vengeance. But I will not leave here without knowing that the man who killed my family is dead."

"How much better," the younger man said, "if you put him through what you experienced. He will return to find his family dead. Strike the dragon by chaining him to the same prison."

"What is your plan?"

"The teams are prepared. We dare not wait until next week."

Dark Man looked around the room, studying the faces. "Are you all agreed?"

They nodded.

"But you were the one willing to stand up to me."

"They voted and I lost."

Laughter filled the room.

"Very well," Dark Man said. "Send the message. No one must know our plans. We will strike with precision. And when children lie dead in their schools, when mothers and fathers weep, our work will be complete."

CHAPTER 35

Bryce

It was fun going to the mailbox every day because I was getting letters back from wallet owners. Some were from soldiers themselves, and others were from family members.

One letter was from a daughter whose father had died overseas. She said the wallet gave her a new perspective of him. *I've seen old pictures and letters, but I can't thank you enough for going to the trouble to send this last link,* she wrote.

I still had Patrick Elkins' wallet left. I'd called his brother almost every day and hadn't reached him. I wondered if he even lived in Idaho anymore.

I had a few minutes before school so I dialed the number. I was about to hang up when a guy answered.

"Mr. Elkins?" I said.

"You got him."

"Are you Patrick Elkins' brother?"

"Yeah, is there a problem with Pat?"

"No, I'm just surprised. I've been trying to reach you for a long time."

"I work the late shift and I sleep during the day. What's up with Patrick?"

I explained what I'd found and asked about Patrick.

"We talk on the phone some, but the last I saw him was almost 10 years ago. I asked if he was ever coming back home, and he said there were too many memories. Our parents died years ago, and about the only connection he had was a lady friend of his—"

"Miss Coleman?"

"How did you know that?" he said.

"It's why I'm trying to reach him."

I heard paper rattling and figured he was digging through a drawer. He finally found his brother's number and gave it to me.

"Thanks, Mr. Elkins."

"No, thank you. Tell the old buzzard I asked about him."

I was about to dial the number when Mom tapped my shoulder and pointed to the clock. "School?"

I grabbed my lunch and backpack and headed for the door.

CHAPTER 36

❀ Ashley ❀

Secret Admirer still had my interest. Maybe I focused on him because I was so disappointed about Duncan and Hayley. Or it could have been because he was so good at staying hidden. I had tried to catch him and even asked others to help (not telling them *why* they should watch my locker), but he was still a mystery. I even searched notebooks for red pens.

The dance was coming up in a week, so he had to show his face soon. I tried to go about my business, but I kept looking around and wandering the halls. I even stayed late to see if he would show up, but I only saw Mr. Patterson.

"Still looking for that mystery guy, huh?" Other than Bryce, he was the only one who knew about my hunt.

"Have you seen anyone suspicious hanging around?"

He shook his head. "Saw your brother a few minutes ago; that's all. Are you going to the dance?"

"Still not sure."

He sighed. "It's going to be a different school without you and Bryce next year. Have any plans for the summer?"

I told him about a possible job at the Toot Toot Café and a trip Mom and Sam had talked about.

Mr. Patterson smiled. "Sounds really nice. You deserve a good summer before high school. You scared?"

"A little. Getting to class on time and all that."

"You'll be fine, I'm sure." A door opened at the office, and Mr. Patterson moved away. "If I see anyone suspicious, I'll let you know."

Mr. Bookman walked toward me. I figured he was upset that I had stayed late, but he smiled as he approached. "Miss Timberline, I just left a message on your answering machine at home. I'm glad I caught you."

"Is something wrong?"

"No, on the contrary, I have wonderful news. Both for you and your brother."

CHAPTER 37

Bryce

"We won?" I said to Ashley as she told us the news. I hung up the phone—I was calling Mr. Elkins, but this news floored me. I wanted to celebrate, but something held me back. "Both of us won? With all the schools in the country? They just finished taking entries a couple of weeks ago."

"Someone from the contest called Mr. Bookman and said we should both be at school Friday."

"So we didn't necessarily win."

"He said contest officials will be there. That's all I know."

I thought about the "borrowed" part of my story. Did I deserve to win? "Maybe we're just in the finals." I looked at Mom. "You think it's a problem that you're a writer? Maybe they think you helped."

"I suggested a happy ending on yours, but I didn't help. And I edited Ashley only a little. I'm sure it's simply a formality."

"Did Mr. Bookman mention that anybody else won?" I said.

Ashley shrugged. "He just said we should be there."

I did a little victory hop around the kitchen, knowing Dylan would join in. He ran in from the living room, grabbed my shirt, and soon we had a four-person conga line, kicking our legs and laughing.

Then Leigh walked in the front door.

I've always imagined what it must have been like to see Jesus calm a storm, but it couldn't have stopped quicker than our dancing after seeing Leigh's face.

"What's wrong, honey?" Mom said. She moved toward her, but Leigh shrank away, holding out a pink piece of paper.

"A speeding ticket?" Mom said.

"You or Dad has to go to court with me."

Mom tried to calm her down. Then she must have seen how fast Leigh was going when she got pulled over.

"The officer said I can get my license taken away." Leigh's chin quivered.

"I have a friend at the town hall who I can ask. Don't worry. One of us will—"

"Face it," Leigh said. "Dad's never coming back. And why would he?" She looked at us. "You're all a bunch of Jesus freaks waiting to pounce on your prey!"

Leigh walked toward Ashley. "Randy told me you guys talked with him about God and all that junk. It's your fault he left me!" She ran upstairs and slammed her door. It was like an explosion in the upstairs hallway.

"What did Ashley and Bryce do wrong, Mama?" Dylan said.

Mom pulled him close and patted his back. He broke away and grabbed my shirt again, but none of us were in the mood to dance.

"She's just upset," Mom said. "Probably why she got the ticket."

My hands sweated as I dialed Patrick Elkins' number later. When a woman answered, my heart sank. I wanted him to be single so he could get back in touch with Velma. I asked about Mr. Elkins, and the woman said he was at church.

"Do you know when your husband will be back?" I said.

"Oh, I'm not his wife. I just clean for him."

Wonderful, I thought.

She wrote my number down, and I stayed by the phone the rest of the evening. Anytime it rang I raced for it.

He called after 8 p.m., and his voice sounded scratchy and older. "This is Patrick Elkins. I was told you wanted to talk with me. Hope it's not too late."

I told him I was in Colorado and what time it was.

"Good, I'm glad I'm not waking anyone up. How old are you, son?"

I told him, then explained about finding the wallet.

He got quiet, thinking things through. "I remember that now. Thought I'd lost it on the train. I knew a couple other fellows who lost theirs too. As I remember, there was a Dear John letter in there from a sweetheart of mine."

"Dear John?"

"It's what we called it. A girl who wanted to break up with a guy."

"You never read it, right?"

"No, but I knew what was in there."

"What if I told you it wasn't a Dear John? that Miss Coleman said she would wait for you?"

He snorted. "I'd say you were snooping."

"Mr. Elkins, I've sent out a lot of wallets. I couldn't locate you, so I called Miss Coleman. She still lives in your hometown. She's never forgotten you, though she said she heard you were married."

"I did marry, but my wife died a few years back." He paused. "You're saying she wasn't dumping me?"

"If you'll give me your address, I'll send it."

He gave me his address, and I told him his brother said hello.

"You've talked to a lot of people trying to find me, haven't you?"

"I couldn't stop. Part of me thinks you and Miss Coleman . . . well, deserve each other."

He chuckled. "What did she say when you asked about me?"

I told him. "Sir, I'm just a kid and I wouldn't dare give you advice, but I'm convinced she's still interested."

"Well, why don't you stop yapping and give me her number?"

I promised I'd send the wallet the next day, and he said he would send some money to cover the mailing expense.

When I hung up, I thought about the contest. I knew I couldn't accept any award I was given.

CHAPTER 38

❀ Ashley ❀

There were a million things I wanted to say to Leigh, but I knew she didn't want to hear any of them. Bryce and I had talked with Randy about spiritual stuff, but we'd never twisted his arm.

The more I stood outside her door and listened to her cry, the more questions I had about my own situation. *What if the whole secret-admirer routine is made up? What if somebody is doing this to be mean?*

Who would want to hurt me like this? Is someone trying to make my life miserable?

Instead of guys, I thought of girls who might have stuck the notes in my locker. Hayley? Marion? But the phone call had been from a guy.

My mind was full of questions, and I finally willed myself to go to the phone. I dialed Hayley's number.

She picked up on the fourth ring. "Oh, hi, Ashley," she said, sounding surprised.

"I need to talk to you."

"Uh . . . I'm on the other line. . . . Can I call you back?"

"You talking with Duncan?"

She paused. "I'll call you back."

I took the phone to my room, closed the door, and looked through the yearbook. *Was it Chuck Burly on the phone? Duncan could have put him up to it. Maybe Hayley and Duncan are working together!*

The phone rang. It was Hayley.

"I know what's going on," I said.

"Listen, Ashley, I'm sorry about Duncan. It just kind of happened, and I didn't know what to say."

"So that's why you're trying to hurt me with this secret-admirer thing?"

"What?"

"All the letters and notes and e-mails. Who'd you get to be your stooge—Chuck? Some high school guy your sister knows?"

"Ashley, I don't know what you're talking about." Her surprise sounded genuine.

"Nothing," I said. "Look, don't worry about Duncan. You two played tennis together last summer and I was fine, remember?"

"Yeah, but that's different than a dance. Are you all right?"

"I'm fine. Thanks for calling back."

CHAPTER 39

Bryce

Sometimes life throws a curveball—you expect one thing and something else happens. Then life throws a fastball that narrowly misses your chin, and you're scared to step into the batter's box.

Well, with the contest, life seemed to be throwing a nice, fat, off-speed pitch right down the middle, while at the same time throwing a beanball to my head.

Ashley and I tried to keep it a secret, but somehow word leaked that our names had been mentioned in the contest. It spread like wildfire, and by lunch people were asking what I'd written.

Marion Quidley sat across from me at lunch and just smiled.

"What?" I said.

"I knew you were award material," she said. "Must have been a really good story."

"I don't want to talk about it."

She opened her lunch bag and dug around inside. "Yeah, that proves it. Artists don't want anyone to know what they're working on."

I excused myself and found Mr. Gminski in his room. He was eating a big sandwich, a pickle, two donuts, and a Diet Coke.

"I need to ask you something."

"What's up?"

"What if I knew somebody who wrote something for a contest, but not everything they wrote was original."

"Plagiarism? Stealing someone else's material?"

"Not all of it was copied, but some of it was. What would happen to that person?"

He chewed his pickle like it was magic and could give him extra thought powers. "If I were a judge, I'd disqualify the entry. If the person had copied material by mistake, I might be more lenient. Was it a mistake?"

"I don't think so."

"Bryce, only two names have been mentioned in regard to this contest—yours and your sister's. As far as I'm concerned, this conversation didn't happen. But if I were you—or the person who did this—I'd contact the judges."

I nodded. "And how would I do that?"

"Talk with Mr. Bookman. He may know where they're staying before they get here tomorrow."

CHAPTER 40

Ashley

I ate lunch by myself and walked through the halls like a zombie. It felt like every friend had abandoned me. Marion wouldn't talk to me because I wouldn't tell her what was going on with my locker. I'd had such high hopes that she would become a Christian, but now that seemed in jeopardy. Of all the people in school, Bryce was the only one who would even look at me.

I stopped in the middle of the hall, kids streaming around, near the science room where the old skeleton hung. Marion said it was a former biology teacher who had donated her body to science.

Bryce, I thought. *What if he's trying to cheer me up and put those notes in my locker? He could be the one! He got me to look at my e-mail. He could have had someone call me, then say he couldn't find anyone at the pay phone!*

Then it clicked. Bryce has a favorite pen in his folder that has blue, black, and *red* ink. And on the day I got one of the notes, Mr. Patterson said he saw Bryce in the hall.

I had to move away from the skeleton; it was unnerving me. I found my next class but couldn't concentrate. Part of me felt betrayed, but another part felt loved. I wanted to hug and slug Bryce at the same time.

What is he thinking? How will this end?

CHAPTER 41

Bryce

I went to the front office to find Mr. Bookman and spotted Ashley. She saw me and gave me a weird look. I asked what was wrong, but she shook her head.

"Figure out who the guy is?" I said.

She stared at me. "I have a pretty good idea."

"Who?"

She walked out the front door.

"Hey, what's wrong? What did I say?"

I figured she'd just had a bad day so I let her go. I spotted Mr. Bookman getting his jacket and hat. "Mr. Bookman, I was wondering—"

"Mr. Timberline, I am late for a dental appointment and my molars are killing me, so if you'll excuse me . . ."

I walked beside him out of the office. "I was wondering if you knew the judge's name from the contest."

He chuckled. "Excited, huh?"

"Sort of. Do you know the name?"

"Something Smith, I think. There's a call slip on my desk with his information."

"Is he in town?"

"I'm not sure." We were at his car. "I need to go. Relax. Friday will be here soon enough."

"Can I see that slip of paper?" I said.

He looked at his watch. "All right. Tell my secretary you can copy the number, but don't be a pest to this man."

"Thanks, Mr. Bookman."

I walked toward the entrance and noticed Ashley standing by the bike rack. "What's wrong now?"

She didn't even look at me. "I know it was you."

"What?"

She turned, and it was like one of those scary-movie commercials. A person swivels their head around, and you see an alien growing out of their ear or something. It makes you not sleep for a week. "I know *you're* my secret admirer," she said.

My laughter was like the Whos' in Who-ville. It started out low and began to grow. I held my stomach as my face turned red.

"Stop," Ashley said.

"I can't! That's the funniest thing I've ever heard. You think *I* want to go to the dance with *you*?"

She tried to explain the clues, but I told her it wasn't me. "Honest, Ash."

That seemed to satisfy her, and she walked back into the office with me. I was glad because the secretary doesn't care for boys. I explained what Mr. Bookman said, but it wasn't until Ashley confirmed my story (she'd heard the whole thing) that the secretary got the slip from his desk.

"Copy this number and give it back, okay?" she said, handing me a pink slip.

I read the slip.

To: *Principal Bookman*
Fr: *Jeffrey Smith*
Re: *Writing contest—*
wants to interview winners this Friday.
Call his cell at 555-3431.

I wrote down the information and thanked her. She didn't look up. She just took the slip as if I were a seal returning a fish.

I dialed the number, but a message said the subscriber was unavailable. There was no way to leave a message.

"Just wait until Friday to talk to him," Ashley said.

There are some things you can tell your sister and some things you keep to yourself. I didn't want anyone knowing what I'd done.

"If it's so important, go down to the Red Rock Inn," Ashley said. "If he's staying in town, he has to be there."

CHAPTER 42

❀ Ashley ❀

A warm breeze hit us as Bryce and I walked toward the Red Rock Inn. At this time of year, the grass grows like crazy and flowers bloom and the air is fresh. I tried to forget I'd just accused my twin of writing me notes and concentrated on the contest man. The way Bryce acted, it seemed important to find him.

The Red Rock Inn sits on a knoll a few blocks from school. This is the closest place to stay overnight, unless you drive to Castle Rock or Colorado Springs.

Today the lot was full, and Bryce pointed at the sign. It said Welcome Air Force Families!

"It's graduation at the academy, so they're probably full," Bryce said.

That explained all the airplanes zooming overhead, getting ready for the ceremony. I'd heard on the radio that the vice president was supposed to give the main address.

The lobby was cozy with nice couches and chairs. Paperback books lined a shelf, and a sign said Give One—Take One. One room had tables and a small breakfast area, where people could get donuts, oatmeal, toast, and cereal. All that had been put away, but there were a few pieces of fruit left for stragglers.

There were two people at the front desk, and I sat and read a paper while Bryce asked for help. One of the headlines on the front page said "Terror Alert Stalls DIA." It was a story about Denver International Airport and how slow things had gotten since the new terror alert.

I was engrossed in a Life section story on a movie star who had adopted four children from Thailand when Bryce came over, frowning. "He said there's no Jeffrey Smith staying here."

"Maybe he's not coming until tomorrow," I said.

"He said there's no reservation under that name for the rest of the week."

"Must be staying in the Springs. Let's call around."

CHAPTER 43

Bryce

As Ashley and I walked away from the motel, I noticed most cars had Air Force bumper stickers. Then I spotted something weird. Parked in the last row, slightly off the pavement in some pine trees, was the van I'd seen around town. I told Ashley I'd catch up with her, and she headed home.

I ran down the knoll into the trees and glanced around for anyone who might be watching. Everything looked clear. I tried the doors to the van, but they were locked. I couldn't see into the back because there were no windows, but the front was messy and filled with maps. One sat open on the dashboard, near a huge crack in the windshield. I stepped onto the running board to get a better look. It was a map of Texas with a route highlighted going north. There was writing in the margin that almost looked like another language.

I noticed folded maps for California, Arizona, and Florida on top of another pile. There must have been 30 stuffed into the island between the front seats.

I stepped back and looked at the sign on the door. It was for a paint shop located a few blocks from the center of town.

I was writing down the address when someone with a high-pitched voice shouted, "Get away from that van!" A curly-headed man with a beard ran toward me.

I moved slowly into the pine trees, but when I saw how angry the guy was, I ran. I passed the duck pond behind the library, where the cross-country team had jogged a million times. I knew a shortcut to the other side and made it while the guy shook his fist and yelled.

CHAPTER 44

❀ Ashley ❀

I heard Mom laughing as soon as I got in the door. She was on the phone, waving from the couch. "It's Carolyn's mom from Chicago." Then she laughed some more. I don't know about you, but I get a good feeling when I hear an adult really laugh.

I grabbed some munchies from the pantry and sat by her. (I can never wait until dinner, and that bugs Mom.) She asked about Tim, Carolyn's brother. When Bryce and I had visited in the fall, Tim was wild, but I could tell by Mom's face that he was doing a lot better. Mom told me later that the whole family was doing better, including Larry and Peggy, who had gotten married before Christmas.

"You want to talk to Carolyn before I hang up?" she said.

"Sure," I said.

I took the phone to my room to talk. It felt good to laugh and tell her about my secret admirer. When I told her about the writing contest, she gasped.

"I can't believe you have a winner too," Carolyn said. "Today they made an announcement at my school encouraging everyone to be there Friday."

"Do you know who won?" I said.

"No, they just wanted all of us to show up. Isn't it exciting?"

"They sure work fast," I said.

"You know these contests," Carolyn said. "They know the kind of stuff they're looking for. Well, good luck. I hope you take first place."

CHAPTER 45

Bryce

My legs burned as I ran into town. I kept looking around, waiting for Curly Hair to jump me, but he never showed.

I called home, but Mom must have been on the line. The phone just rang and rang.

Since I was here, I figured I'd look for the painter's office, and I found it—a small, run-down house that looked like it needed a fresh coat of paint. I think they call that irony. The driveway was empty, and the lights were off inside. I rang the doorbell and knocked, but no one answered. I looked in the front window and saw cans of paint stacked against a wall.

The front window was open a little, and a phone with a blinking red light sat on a desk. I was about to leave when the phone rang.

An older woman left a message. "Ernie, this is Shirley Potts—I thought we were scheduled to work on my front room today. Can you call me so we can reschedule? Or maybe I had it wrong." She gave her number and hung up.

The guy who had chased me from the van didn't strike me as an Ernie, but I guess stranger things have happened.

"What are you doing, kid?" someone said behind me. It was a man next door. He wore a T-shirt and sweatpants.

"I was looking for the owner. Have you seen him?"

"Haven't seen him in a couple of days."

"Does he have curly hair and a beard?"

The man laughed. "He hasn't had curly hair for 30 years. He hasn't had *any* hair for 30 years."

"So he's not a middle-aged guy, kind of skinny?"

"Nope. Has a belly out to here. Why do you ask?"

"I saw a van with his company name on it and wondered."

"Maybe Ernie went on vacation and has subcontractors doing his work. Didn't tell me anything about it, but he pretty much keeps to himself."

I thanked him and walked back toward the motel. The days were getting longer and the sunsets more spectacular. The sky was bright orange when I reached the pine trees on the south side of the motel. I could see the room Curly Hair had come out of and the van from here.

Nothing happened for a while. Then a car with Texas plates backed in near the van and parked. The driver was short with olive skin. The passenger was a little taller, with short hair and dark eyebrows. He walked like a lion that had just eaten a wildebeest.

As they approached the motel, Curly Hair came out and hugged Mr. Lion. Three more guys surrounded them; then two doors opened and others joined the group. This wasn't any Air Force get-together.

Curly Hair pointed at the van and held out his hands like he was pleading for something.

Mr. Lion shook his head and stalked inside.

Something about Mr. Lion looked familiar. I was sure I'd seen him somewhere before, but where?

Curly Hair headed to the van, and my cell phone rang. Before I could answer, he ran toward me.

CHAPTER 46

❀ Ashley ❀

Bryce picked up his phone but didn't answer. All I heard was scratching and bouncing, like he was running.

"Bryce?" I said.

No answer. Just heavy breathing. Then a man shouted.

"Bryce!"

"Ash, I can't talk. I'll call as soon as I'm safe."

"Where's your brother?" Mom said as she put dinner on the table.

"He'll be home in a while. He called when I was on the phone with Carolyn, but I think he was checking in."

"You two up to something?" she said.

"Why do you say that?"

She looked over the top of her glasses, and I smiled. She does that when she knows there's something up.

The phone rang a few minutes later just as Dylan began his vegetable war with Mom. Dylan wanted to eat Mike and Ikes instead of peas and corn.

"Those are for dessert," Mom said as I picked up the phone.

"I'll eat the green ones," Dylan protested.

"Hello?" I said.

Bryce was out of breath. "Ash, remember that van I told you about? The one I saw at school and the house?" His voice echoed, like he was inside a jar.

"Bryce, where are you?"

"Just listen. I think something's going on with these guys at the motel."

"Are they with the contest?"

"I don't know." He told me about his trip into town and getting chased.

"With all that excitement, you probably don't want to know what I found out about Jeffrey Smith," I said.

"What?"

"I called 12 different hotels on the north side of the Springs. None of them have a Jeffrey Smith or a reservation for him. Guess you'll have to wait until Friday. Why'd you want to see him so bad, anyway?"

"It's personal," he said. "I gotta go. See you soon."

CHAPTER 47

Bryce

I sat in the library bathroom and waited. I figured Curly Hair wouldn't bother me here. What did he have to hide?

I slipped out and moved through the nonfiction stacks, looking out the window at ducks crossing the parking lot. Kids and parents tossed bread.

I hung around a little longer, looking at books and DVDs. I was about to leave when I heard a commotion outside. A white blur streaked past the windows, and someone screamed. I circled the building and found a girl sobbing. Several people gathered around a lump on the pavement. Feathers were everywhere.

"He just ran over it without stopping!" the girl cried.

"Did anybody get his license-plate number?" someone said.

"The license was covered with mud," the father said.

I spotted the white van heading for the interstate. Someone from the library brought a heavy trash bag and a shovel.

I ran to the motel to get a better look. I waited until the sun went down, staying in the shadows. I could see the flicker of the television inside. I was getting hungry and about to head home when an old car rattled into the parking lot. A guy in a Pizza Hut shirt carried six boxes and knocked on Mr. Lion's door.

I moved closer, trying to hear them, but the door closed. The pizza guy turned, and I recognized him. It was Danny Ingram, a guy Ashley and I had helped about a year earlier. I'd heard he was living with his parents again, but I didn't know he had a job.

"Hey," I said, hoping he'd remember me.

"Yeah, how's it going? Bryce, right?"

I nodded. "Lot of pizzas in that room. They give you a good tip?"

"Not bad. At least one guy in there spoke English."

"What do you mean?"

"You know, Middle Eastern types having a party. Well, I gotta make another run."

"You're not going toward my house, are you?"

"As a matter of fact, I am headed that way. You need a ride?"

"Great."

I hopped in, then remembered Mom's rule about getting rides from people. I called and got permission.

As Danny drove, I tried to look at the order slip from the motel, but he had it in his pocket.

"Who was that guy in the motel? You get a name?"

He pulled the slip from his pocket. "Johnson. Bill Johnson."

He let me out at my driveway, and I thanked him. Smith. Johnson. Something didn't make sense.

PART 3

CHAPTER 48

❀ Ashley ❀

You could sense the excitement that Thursday morning. A few kids had left on vacation, but most were making plans. There were more bikes in the racks than ever. Girls whispered about the dance, less than a week away, talking about dresses and hair. Some had appointments at salons.

I didn't know what to wear or if I should even go. I still didn't know who my secret admirer was.

Skeeter Messler caught up with me in the hall, just past the principal's office. "I guess tomorrow is the big day—finding out about the contest," he said.

"Yeah," I said.

"Do you have a date for the dance?"

I shook my head. "Still not sure."

His eyes were like flies, looking at his shoes, the wall, down the hall, then finally they landed on me. "I'll get two tickets in case. Okay?"

Now *my* eyes were flies. I closed them, then looked at him. "That's really sweet, Skeeter, but I'm probably not going. Why don't you ask Marion?"

His eyes were dead flies. "Thanks for the tip, Ashley."

"I didn't mean to—," I said, but he disappeared in a sea of eighth graders.

The "circle of love" amazes me. One person likes another, but that person likes someone who doesn't like them, and on and on. When two people actually find each other, they usually get too close and bad things happen.

I walked to my locker, hoping high school wouldn't be this hard. I opened it and a slip of paper fluttered to the floor. My heart skipped a beat. It was pretty stationery—flowers around the edges. Taped inside was a peel-off smiley face.

Dear Ashley,

I'm sorry it's taken so long to tell you who I am. I keep thinking that when you find out, you'll walk away. My mom told me that wasn't true, but I'm not sure.

I noticed you rode your bike today, so meet me behind the climbing wall after school. Put this sticker on your locker to show you'll be there.

You have made a big impact on my life. I hope I can return the favor.

Sincerely,
Your Secret Admirer

I read the note again, observing that he'd learned to spell *sincerely.* How could someone who wrote this be anything but nice? I stuck the smiley face on the front of my locker.

CHAPTER 49

Bryce

At lunch Ashley was as nervous as a rat in a D-Con factory. I asked what was wrong, and she shrugged.

I called the Red Rock Inn and asked for Bill Johnson or Jeffrey Smith, but the desk worker came up empty again.

The Air Force graduation ceremony was that afternoon, and Mrs. Ferguson let us go outside. Parachutists trailed smoke, and there was just about every airplane you could imagine. One was huge and flew so low that I could see the pilot.

"There's the Stealth," someone said as a black triangle-shaped craft soared above us.

An experimental plane shot past us and curved around the red rocks. The whole school shook as the engines flared.

As we walked back inside, I noticed a car parked on the other side of the street. Parents sometimes park there, but it was too early. A dark-haired woman was in the driver's seat, and someone else sat in the passenger seat.

When I got back to class, I looked out the window. The two were still there, talking. Then I realized it was the same car that had been parked near the van at the motel. I noticed two sparkles in the sun and saw the woman holding binoculars.

Strange. I'd heard of divorced parents nabbing their own kids. Or maybe they wanted to kidnap a rich kid and hold him for ransom.

I put the blinds down, telling myself to relax. Sometimes when my mind wanders I can think someone is robbing a bank when they're actually getting a car wash. There had to be a rational, easy explanation about the car.

"Since I just let you watch that aerial display," Mrs. Ferguson said, "I'm going to ask for one more homework assignment."

There were groans around the room.

"I want 500 words on what you just saw. Pick out one plane and describe it or the whole show. Make up a name of a pilot and tell me about him. Whatever you want." She looked at me. "This will be easier for some than others."

I wondered if Mrs. Ferguson knew what I'd done. Had Mr. Gminski talked with her?

CHAPTER 50

❀ Ashley ❀

I brushed my hair and put on lip gloss before last period. I don't use much makeup because it's a pain, but I hate chapped lips.

During class I tried to concentrate, but I kept looking out the window, checking the clock, and sweating. I watched the second hand of the clock tick like that counter on the program *24*, and when the bell rang I actually jumped. I took a deep breath and headed out of the building.

"Ashley," someone whispered. I looked around but didn't see anyone. "Over here!"

It was Bryce, standing behind the cafeteria door.

"What are you doing hiding—?"

"Quiet," he hissed. He grabbed my arm and pulled me behind the door. He peeked through the opening, looking at the office. "Bookman's with a man and a woman. They were looking at the school with binoculars."

"What?"

"Their car was parked at the motel last night."

"It's not the creep you told me about, is it?" I said. "The one who runs over ducks?"

Bryce shook his head.

Mr. Bookman looked like he was talking with the king and queen of some foreign country. "Right this way. We have an auditorium that will seat the whole student body—is that what you're looking for?"

"Yes," the woman said. She had a voice deeper than most guys, husky and gravelly. "We want the whole school to see our presentation."

Bryce pulled me back as they passed.

"That has to be Mr. Smith—didn't you want to talk to him?" I whispered.

"Yeah, but does that guy look like a 'Smith' to you? And why wasn't he listed at the motel?"

I rolled my eyes. "You can't judge people on how they look or what their names are. Anyway, you're on your own. I'm meeting somebody."

CHAPTER 51

Bryce

When Ashley left, I followed Mr. Bookman and the couple to the auditorium. I ran down a back hall and almost knocked Mr. Patterson into his mop and bucket.

He furrowed his brow. "What's the hurry, Timberline?"

"Sorry, Mr. Patterson. Won't happen again."

I handed him the mop he had dropped and moved to the backstage entrance. Mr. Bookman was with the man and woman onstage, pointing out the sound system.

"Impressive," the woman said. "This should work nicely. Will it hold all the teachers and staff? We want them here as well."

The man spoke, and I recognized his voice from the motel. Mr. Lion. "Yes, perhaps the gymnasium would be better suited for this."

"We had 13 schools here for a forensics tournament. There won't be any problem with seating." Mr. Bookman cleared his throat. "Is it true that we have two winners in the school?"

"For legal reasons we can't say until tomorrow," the woman said. "I'm sure you won't be disappointed."

"Do you have a custodian on the premises?" Mr. Smith said.

"Certainly. Let me get him." Mr. Bookman walked away.

The two whispered something about sight lines and exits.

Then Mr. Bookman changed direction and came backstage. "I think he's back here." He walked past me and turned. "Mr. Timberline! How fortuitous. You should meet Mr. and Mrs. Smith from the contest."

"Timberline?" Mrs. Smith said.

CHAPTER 52

❀ Ashley ❀

Call it nerves or lack of courage, but I didn't go straight to the climbing wall. I stood near the flagpole, watching out of the corner of my eye.

When the parking lot was empty and the only bikes left were Bryce's and mine, I moved slowly toward the wall. I was about 20 yards from it when someone called my name. I spun around and saw Marion Quidley.

"Hey," she said. "Why are you still here?"

"Just getting ready to go home," I said. "What about you?"

"I'm meeting my parents at the doctor's office."

"Is your dad okay?" I said.

She smiled. "Yeah. He went to a specialist in Denver—the insurance company wouldn't let him for a long time. Anyway, they found something in his blood and started a new treatment. He's been feeling a lot better. They say if he keeps improving, he can go back to work this summer."

I couldn't believe it. "That's great!" I hugged her.

"Look, I'm sorry about the way I've treated you," Marion said. "For ignoring you. I think I'm ready . . ." She paused and looked behind me. "Who's that behind the climbing wall?"

I turned and saw an elbow sticking out, but I couldn't see his face. Whoever it was wore a short-sleeved shirt. "I don't know. You're ready for what?"

"Church . . . you know, a Bible study or something. I want to start learning. Could you help me?"

I told her my mom was thinking about starting a study with a few teenage girls in the neighborhood.

"Count me in." She looked at her watch. "Gotta get to the doctor's office. See you tomorrow!"

I turned my back to her and took a huge breath. This day was turning out better than I thought. I took a step. The guy was leaning against the other side of the wall, one tennis shoe exposed.

Could it be Duncan?

I was a few feet from the wall when Mr. Bookman yelled, "Miss Timberline!" He was at the front door, waving. "Mr. and Mrs. Smith would like a word with you. Your brother said you were still here."

I looked back at the wall, hoping my secret admirer would step out.

"Miss Timberline!" Mr. Bookman said.

I hurried back inside the school.

CHAPTER 53

Bryce

"Are you excited about tomorrow?" Mrs. Smith said to me when Mr. Bookman went for Ashley. I had asked him to get her so I could have time alone with these two.

"I need to tell you something about my entry."

"And what is that?" she said.

"In my story, where the letter shows up . . ."

"We don't actually read the submissions," Mr. Smith said. "That's done by others."

"All right, there's a part of my story that's a letter, and I basically copied it word for word."

They looked at each other.

"I want to withdraw the entry. It wouldn't be right."

Mr. Smith threw back his head and laughed. His wife did too.

"What's so funny?" I said.

Just then Mr. Patterson came through the door, his keys jangling. "Mr. Bookman said you wanted to see me?"

"Yes. If you wouldn't mind, we'd like a tour of the school after we've spoken with our winners."

Mr. Patterson looked at me and smiled. "You bet. I'll be down the hall."

Before I could talk more about my story, Mr. Bookman and Ashley came down the aisle.

"Congratulations, Miss Timberline," Mr. Smith said. "You and your brother should be very proud of your accomplishment."

"So we won?" Ashley said, surprised.

"Yes. Most schools are lucky to have one person in the top 10, but your *family* has two first-place winners."

Ashley couldn't help smiling. "What's going to happen tomorrow?"

Mr. Smith explained that we'd all meet in the auditorium at 9 a.m. "We'd appreciate it if you keep this news to yourself—and your parents, of course. Will they be here?"

"Our mom can," Ashley said, "but our dad's away."

"Oh, that's too bad," Mrs. Smith said. "If he knows, maybe he could return?"

"I don't think so. He's in Washington right now . . ."

I nudged her, and she gave me a look like she was going to rip out my spleen. Sam told us never to talk to anyone about his trips.

". . . but we could call him and ask," she finished.

"Yes, please. I'm sure your father won't want to miss this."

Ashley walked out, but I stayed. Mr. Bookman offered to give the Smiths a tour, but the two said Mr. Patterson would do that.

"About what I told you earlier," I said when we were alone. "I don't deserve an award for something I—"

Mr. Smith put a finger to his lips. "Trust me. No one will know. You should see how many parents write their children's essays. Because of your honesty, and because it was only part of the story, we'll call it creative license."

Mrs. Smith put a hand on my shoulder. "Don't be concerned. Go home and call your father. Your whole family should share your achievement."

I walked into the hall with them, then split off as they found Mr. Patterson.

CHAPTER 54

❀ Ashley ❀

I hurried outside toward the climbing wall. Some kids played soccer in a nearby field; otherwise the place was deserted. I put a hand on the wall, took a breath, and walked to the other side. No one was there. I almost cried.

I noticed something at the bottom. It was a single rose and another note.

> Ashley,
>
> I thought I heard you, but when I looked, you were gone. I guess you changed your mind. Or maybe you found out who I am.

I guess this wasn't meant to be. Here's the rose I was saving for you. I hope you like it.

S. A.

I took the rose and trudged to my bike. Then a thought struck me. I put the rose gently inside my backpack and pulled out a pen and paper. I wrote a hasty note and walked to my locker.

Mr. Bookman came out as I was going in. "I think your brother has already left."

"Thanks. I just wanted to put this in my locker."

He smiled. "Yes, well, I'll allow it this time. We're very proud of you, Ashley. I hope you know that."

I wanted to ask him if he was proud enough to let us ride our ATVs to school, but I didn't.

I went to my locker, my footsteps echoing eerily off the walls. It felt like someone was going to jump out at me. I taped the note to the front of my locker, hoping Secret Admirer would see it. If I got to school early enough tomorrow, I could still find out who he was.

CHAPTER 55

Bryce

I was halfway home when I turned around. The Smiths had talked me into taking the prize, but I didn't deserve it. When I got back to school, I met Ashley. "Why aren't you riding your bike?"

She looked lost in thought. "I forgot." Then she snapped out of it. "What are *you* doing back here?"

"I have to talk to that Smith guy again." Then the whole story came out about what I'd done. It felt good telling someone. Especially someone who cared for me. "I don't feel right about accepting the prize."

Ashley said she understood and followed me back to the school. The door was locked, but Mr. Smith's car was still parked in front. Strange.

"Maybe they walked to the motel," she said. "It's not that far."

We rode our bikes to the motel. "Hey, there's Mr. Patterson's car," Ashley said. It was parked at the back, near the pines.

"Ash, something strange is going on. Mr. Patterson stays a long time after school's out."

"So what could be happening?"

"I don't know, but something about Mr. Smith and that lady bothers me. They made a big deal about having Mom and Sam at the ceremony tomorrow."

Two Middle Eastern men came out of Mr. Smith's room carrying black equipment boxes. The boxes looked heavy. They put them in a minivan and drove away.

"See? This thing gets weirder every minute." I snapped my fingers and pulled out my phone.

"What are you doing?"

I dialed the motel office and asked for Mr. Smith's room number. It rang twice before he answered.

"Mr. Smith, this is Bryce Timberline."

"Oh, Bryce, yes," he said. "I hope you haven't changed your mind."

"No, it's not that. I left something at school. Do you know where Mr. Patterson is?"

"Hmm, we left some time ago. He did mention that he was meeting someone, but I don't know where."

"Why is your car still at the school?"

He chuckled. "Inquisitive, aren't you? My wife and I decided to walk. It's such a nice afternoon." He put a hand over the phone and said something to someone. "Is there something wrong, Mr. Timberline?"

I told Ashley to hit the dirt. Just then a door opened and someone came outside.

"Bryce, are you still there?" Mr. Smith said.

I hung up and scooted back, pulling Ashley with me. We raced through the trees to our bikes and rode straight home.

CHAPTER 56

❀ Ashley ❀

Bryce was right. Something was out of place with the Smiths—including the fact that neither wore a wedding band. But what? Maybe all contest people are a little weird.

Mom was excited about the news and said she would definitely be at school. "I don't think Sam can make it. He is flying today, but I don't know where."

I didn't tell her anything about Bryce's story. I figured he would tell Mom if he wanted.

Bryce had a far-off stare at dinner and didn't laugh when Dylan burped. It was a long, loud one too, because Dylan was drinking root beer.

"Something wrong, honey?" Mom said to Bryce. "Ashley said you both won."

He gave me a glance, then said, "I was just thinking of Chuck Burly. Could I go over to his house to play video games? He has a new one."

"Your homework done?"

Bryce nodded. "Had to write about some planes. And maybe I could stay overnight?"

"We'll see about that," she said. "Go ahead and call him."

Chuck's house is past the school, and I figured Bryce wanted another look. I followed him to the phone. "You and I both know you're not going to Chuck's house."

"Yes, I am. I talked with him today—not about sleeping over, but he's got a new—"

"You want to look at the school again or the motel, right?"

"I'm curious, okay? Anything wrong with that?"

He left a few minutes later. Then the phone rang, and it was Carolyn calling for me. "I just heard from a friend. We definitely have a winner in our school. They announce it tomorrow."

"Same here," I said. "Do you know who it is?"

"No, they wouldn't say. I think they want a big crowd."

I told her that Bryce and I had won, and she squealed with delight. "I'll call you after school," she said. "Our assembly starts at 10 tomorrow morning."

CHAPTER 57

Bryce

The sun dipped below the mountains as I parked my ATV at Mrs. Watson's place and walked past the school. There was a light on inside, which was strange.

I noticed the minivan from the motel and the Smiths' car in the school parking lot. I went around behind the climbing wall and tried to see inside, but most windows had shades drawn.

I walked all the way around the school and didn't see anything inside. I moved behind some bushes in the front and heard shouting. I pulled on the front-door handle, but it was locked. Keys hung in the lock, which was something Mr. Patterson would never do.

I sat, catching my breath, when I heard footsteps. It was Skeeter Messler carrying his chess board. I ran to him.

He seemed surprised. "What are you doing here, Timberline?"

I shrugged and laughed, and that seemed to satisfy him.

"Your sister figure out who was sending those love notes?"

"Don't think so," I said, surprised he knew about it.

He thought for a moment. "Who are *you* taking to the dance?"

"Don't know if I'm going," I said. I had thought of asking Lynette.

The front door opened, and I moved Skeeter around the corner so we wouldn't be seen. I was dying to see who was behind us.

"Think you could give me some help with your sister? I tried convincing her to go with me—"

"Let me talk to her when I get home."

"Why are you whispering?"

"Just waiting for someone," I said.

"Have her call me, would you?"

"Sure, Skeeter."

He cut across the graveled lot and disappeared into the trees.

I looked around the corner and saw the front door closing. I scurried to the sign our class had bought for the school. It said Eighth-Grade Dance Next Wednesday. Pretty soon it would say Have a Great Summer!

CHAPTER 58

Ashley

Mom asked me to watch Dylan while she ran to the store. Leigh came in and went to her room. I wanted to tell her about the contest and ask about Randy, but it's hard to talk to a blur.

Dylan said he was bored, so I dug through his closet and found an electric car. With fresh batteries installed, he used it to chase Pippin and Frodo around the living room until they jumped onto the couch. They watched it go round and round like two NASCAR fans.

The phone rang, and I was surprised to hear Sam. There was airplane noise in the background. I asked if he could come to the assembly tomorrow.

"Don't think so. Can you have someone videotape it?"

I told him Mom would and hoped he could sense my disappointment. "Have you found out any more about the attack?"

"We've picked up more chatter. Don't worry, though. We'll catch these guys, and things will get back to normal."

CHAPTER 59

Bryce

The wind picked up and it was getting chilly, but I was determined to keep watching the door. I wanted to make sure Mr. Patterson was okay.

I dialed Chuck's house with my cell phone. "I don't think I'm going to make it tonight. Something has come up."

"You okay?" Chuck said.

"Yeah, I'm just going to have to take a rain check on the video game."

The front door opened, and I said good-bye. Curly Hair got into the minivan and raced away.

I ran to the front door. *Unlocked!*

I slipped inside and tiptoed to the cafeteria. It was eerie being in the school alone. At least I hoped I was alone.

The familiar squeaky wheels of Mr. Patterson's cart echoed down the hall, and I looked through the little window in the door. Instead of Mr. Patterson, a man in dark clothing headed for the auditorium. The scene sent a chill down my spine.

When he turned a corner, I followed, sneaking into the auditorium through the open door. Three guys worked above the stage, stringing something behind the curtains. Could they be doing this for the ceremony? Where was Mr. Patterson?

A cell phone rang. "What?" one man said. "Where? . . . Are you sure he came inside? All right, I'll take care of it." He stepped away from the ladder and shouted in another language. I ducked behind a curtain at the back. A lock clicked down the hall—the front door. Men ran past and shouts echoed in the hall.

I held my breath as a man stood in the open door nearby. His cell phone rang again. "We are not sure, sir. We are searching now. . . . Yes, I understand. . . . Yes, of course we've taken care of the janitor. . . . That's not necessary, but—" he paused—"we would be honored to have you here, sir."

I stood, glued to the wall. People ran back and forth, yelling.

A few minutes later, someone unlocked the front door, and I heard Mr. Smith's voice. "If they saw him come inside, he is here."

"Why don't we just go to their home—?"

"No, the father is my main target. We will draw him here."

"Sir, I respect you, but you know this is much bigger than—"

A gun clicked, and Mr. Smith spoke in anger. "Don't ever talk to me that way. Do you understand?"

"Yes . . ."

"You know nothing. The mission will be accomplished, but this man belongs to me. Do you understand?"

"Yes," the other man said.

The group moved into the auditorium. "We have wired it to your specifications. The explosives run behind the curtain to the back."

I noticed something above me—black tape securing a wire to the wall. The wire ran into a brown lump wrapped with more tape, then snaked to another brown lump 15 feet away.

I wasn't sure what was going on, but I knew I had to get out of the school and call the police. Slowly, an idea formed. If I could get into the hall and head out the back, I could run for the culvert that runs under I-25 and lose these guys.

When the men walked into the hall, I took a breath, clenched my fists, and prepared to run. Just as I was about to spring from my hiding place, my phone rang.

"In the auditorium!" Mr. Smith shouted.

I bolted from the shadows and ran into the hall. I knew the alarm would scream when I hit the back door, but I had an even better idea. I pulled the fire alarm as I passed and flew from the building.

I took out my cell phone to dial 911, but Curly Hair jumped in front of me, pointing a gun. He grabbed my phone and yelled, "Back inside!"

Mr. Smith and two other men met us. "So good of you to drop by early, Mr. Timberline." He took my phone from Curly Hair. "Take him downstairs and bring the janitor. Hurry!"

CHAPTER 60

❀ Ashley ❀

The phone rang as I watched the latest reality show. It was so addictive I couldn't pull myself away.

"Ashley, it's for you," Mom said.

I watched the TV as I grabbed the phone. There was no voice on the other end, just wind and a car passing.

"Hello?"

"Ashley, I had to call you one more time."

I focused on his voice. "Who *are* you?"

"You still don't know? I thought you left because you saw me."

"No. I've been trying to figure it out."

"Look, the dance is next week. We should meet tomorrow morning."

Call waiting sounded in my ear. The caller ID said it was Sam on his cell phone.

"I have one more rose," Secret Admirer said. "I'll carry it to the assembly—"

"Hang on a minute. I have to take another call. Stay right there." I hit the button. "Sam?"

"Ashley, I need to talk with your mother."

"I'm on the other line with—"

"Ashley, I *have* to talk with your mother right now," Sam said. I'd never heard him use this tone before. His voice was tight.

"Okay, I'll get her." I found Mom and handed her the phone. "It's Sam, but I'm still on my call."

I stood in the kitchen, watching the reality show and listening.

"No, Bryce is at a sleepover. He's—" Sam must have cut her off. "Okay, I won't say anything. . . . Sam, you're scaring me." That scared me too. "Yes, I'll turn it on now." Mom went into the closet and grabbed her cell phone.

"You hung up!" I said.

"Ashley, grab Dylan. We have to get out of the house."

CHAPTER 61

Bryce

Somewhere between cuffing me with plastic strips and the fire trucks arriving, their plan changed. Curly Hair shoved me into the office while another guy brought Mr. Patterson. The janitor turned off the alarm in the office, and Mr. Smith grabbed him.

"Get rid of them," Mr. Smith hissed. "Say anything about us and the boy dies. If they come inside, you all die."

Mr. Patterson nodded, then wiped blood from his lip and ran a hand over a bump on the back of his head.

"No mistakes," Mr. Smith said.

Mr. Patterson fixed his collar, tucked in his shirt, and opened the door. "Sorry about that, fellows. I was working late and tripped the alarm. I reset it, but I forgot to call."

Curly Hair's grip on me tightened, and the whole thing started to come together for me. I closed my eyes and asked God to get Mr. Patterson and me out of this alive.

The firemen left, and the men used plastic cuffs on Mr. Patterson's wrists. Curly Hair pushed us both to the basement door. Mr. Patterson tumbled downstairs and hit his head so hard that I thought he might be dead.

I turned to Mr. Smith and sneered. "You're not part of the contest—you never have been."

He tilted his head, and something flashed in my mind—a memory I'd carried for years. The man who had shot down my father's plane, whose face had been in every newspaper in the world . . .

"Your name's not Smith. You're Asim bin Asawe."

He smiled and held up my cell phone. "Call your mother and tell her to pick you up here."

"No."

He pulled a gun and pointed it at Mr. Patterson. "Call your mother or he dies."

I clenched my teeth. "She thinks I'm at a sleepover. I'm supposed to be there all night. If I call her, she'll know something's up."

Asim bin Asawe turned the phone off and headed upstairs.

CHAPTER 62

❀ Ashley ❀

Mom dialed Bryce's cell phone and didn't get an answer.

"I don't understand!" Leigh yelled as Mom drove from the house. "What did my dad say?"

Dylan shifted in his car seat, reaching for something. "Where's my blanket? I need my blanket."

Mom looked in the rearview mirror. "We have to get Bryce and then go to a hotel."

"Why?" Leigh said. "I have plans for tomorrow."

"Leigh, I can't explain. You just have to trust me."

"I'm sick of trusting people. And I'm sick of hearing people say I should trust them. When people—"

"Leigh!" Mom shouted. I'd never heard her talk to Leigh like that. "We're in danger. Sam is looking out for us, but you have to—"

"Where is he?" I said.

"Close. They've traced a cell of terrorists to our area. Sam said they may know his true identity."

"How could they have found that out?" I said.

"I don't know," Mom said. "He said something about running a test on our phone. They may have monitored our calls and our computer."

We pulled up to the Burly house, and I went with Mom.

Mrs. Burly came to the door. She called for her son, saying, "Chuckles?"

Chuck blushed when he saw me. "Bryce isn't here. He said he couldn't make it. I thought he was at home."

Mom dialed Bryce's number again but got his voice mail. "If he calls again, tell him to call my cell number," Mom said to Mrs. Burly.

CHAPTER 63

Bryce

They didn't gag us because we were locked in the basement. The stairwell door was shut tight, and it was dark.

"Who are these people?" Mr. Patterson said.

"Terrorists. The lead guy shot down my dad's plane. My real dad."

"What would a terrorist be doing in Red Rock?"

"I think it has something to do with Sam."

"Your stepdad?"

"Yeah. Unless . . ."

"Unless what?"

"Operation Hamar," I said.

"What?"

"My stepdad used to do counterterrorist stuff. He just heard about something called Operation Hamar but doesn't know what it means."

"I'd like to take a hammer to those guys who banged me on the head." He scooted closer. "Turn around and let me see if I can get you loose." When he tested my cuffs, he said, "My snippers are on my cart, but I think there's a box cutter on the shelf. Can you turn the light on at the top of the stairs?"

"I can try."

It took me a few moments to stand with my hands behind me. Try it sometime. When I reached the top, I used my shoulder to find the switch and flicked it on with the back of my head. Light flooded the stairs and basement.

The back of Mr. Patterson's head was bloody and so was his lip. "If we can find that cutter, we can get out of these and surprise them."

CHAPTER 64

❀ Ashley ❀

Mom sat in the Burlys' driveway, staring. She dialed Bryce's phone again, but it went to voice mail. "Where could he have gone on his ATV?"

"Probably on some little mystery," Leigh said.

I almost ripped into her, but Mom stopped me. "You two were up to something earlier. What's going on?"

I sighed. "Bryce wanted to find the guy organizing the contest so he could . . . talk to him."

"What about?" Leigh said.

"I can't say—"

"Ashley, it's important you tell me everything."

I felt like I was betraying my brother, but I figured Mom was right. I told her about what Bryce had done with the letter and his story.

"So the good little Christian is a plagiarist," Leigh said. "Figures. Christians are phonies."

"That's enough," Mom snapped.

"He felt bad about what he did and wanted to pull out of the competition," I said.

Leigh crossed her arms and rolled her eyes.

"We tracked the contest guy to the Red Rock Inn, and Bryce found some strange stuff."

"Strange how?" Mom said as she backed out of the driveway.

"I want my blanket!" Dylan yelled.

"Oh, why do I have to be part of this family!" Leigh said.

"A guy in one of the rooms chased Bryce. The contest man, Mr. Smith, and his wife were at the school."

Mom gunned the engine and sped toward the Red Rock Inn.

CHAPTER 65

Bryce

We looked through the shelves but couldn't find the box cutter.

"I know it's around here somewhere," Mr. Patterson said.

I spotted a gray tool on the bottom shelf and pointed with my foot. He said that was it, but he couldn't reach it. I couldn't pick it up, but I managed to grab it in my mouth.

"Good job," Mr. Patterson said. "Now we need a screwdriver to get the thing open."

He found a flat-head screwdriver, and we went back to the stairs and sat with our backs to each other. We tried several times before we found a position that let us accomplish the task. When the screw fell to the floor, I gave a muted yell of victory.

Mr. Patterson pulled the razor blade from the tool and told me to hold it tightly. "I'll work my hands back and forth, and you hold it still."

As he worked, I thought about Ashley, Mom, and the others. They had no idea what was going on.

Mr. Patterson yelped a couple of times, but then he'd get back on track. I dropped the blade twice and found it, but the third time it bounced away and I had to turn around. That's when I saw that his hands had been cut and there was blood on the floor.

The door opened at the top of the stairs, and Mr. Patterson and I stared at each other.

CHAPTER 66

❀ Ashley ❀

Mom parked and rushed inside the motel. She came back a few minutes later, her face tight. "They haven't seen Bryce. Where's the room you talked about?"

Leigh shook her head. "I don't know if you should go looking—"

"I'm going to find Bryce," Mom snapped.

She spun the car like a stunt driver, and Dylan giggled as we fishtailed toward the parking lot.

"I think it's that one," I said, pointing.

Mom backed into a space and turned off the engine.

"What are you going to do?" Leigh said. "His ATV isn't here."

"He came here the past couple of days," I said.

Mom opened her door and told us to stay inside. She walked to the door and knocked hard.

The curtain inside parted, then closed. The door opened, and Mrs. Smith stepped outside.

Mom said something, and the woman looked surprised. I was curious and figured Mom wouldn't mind, so I got out and moved toward them.

Mrs. Smith saw me and said, "Ashley, what a nice surprise."

Mom gave me a look, then returned her gaze to the woman. "I want to know where my son is," she said sternly.

Mrs. Smith smiled. "You must be so proud of your children and happy with their accomplishments."

"I'd be a lot happier if I could find Bryce. Where is he?"

"I can assure you he's not here. I don't know why you think—"

"He wanted to talk with you and your husband about his story."

"Yes, I called our office and spoke with one of the readers. They assure me his entry is fine."

"I want to talk to your husband," Mom said.

"He's not here," Mrs. Smith said calmly. "Pizza gives him indigestion. I told him he shouldn't have eaten so much last night, but you know how men are. He should be back from the drugstore any minute. Won't you come in?"

Mom paused and focused on the woman. I heard movement inside the room. "I'm sorry to bother you. Bryce is probably at home. Come on, Ashley."

"I told you to stay in the car," Mom said as we walked to the car.

"Something's really wrong, isn't it?"

"Shh," she said. "Just get in."

Mrs. Smith stayed outside and waved as we pulled away.

"She knows something," Mom said.

"How do you know that?" Leigh said.

"Because when she opened the door, before Ashley ever came up, she called me Mrs. Timberline."

Mom looked in the rearview mirror and gasped. Two headlights pierced the back windshield. "We're being followed."

CHAPTER 67

Bryce

Curly Hair appeared at the top of the stairs. As he descended, Mr. Patterson and I scooted back, covering our activity. When Curly Hair was halfway down, I yelled, "Tell Asim I need to talk with him about my stepdad."

The man squinted, then went back upstairs.

When he was gone, Mr. Patterson looked at me. "If these people are after your stepdad, why are they here instead of your house?"

"I don't know. That's what I want to find out."

"Hide that razor blade," he said. "We can't let him see that."

I sat on the blade.

A few moments later Asim appeared with a bottle of juice from a vending machine. He poured some into my mouth and gave some to Mr. Patterson, then sat on a stair and studied me. "You want to talk?"

"It's about my stepdad. He's not a nice person. He's the one you're after, right?"

"If you have information, I'm ready to listen."

"First, let Mr. Patterson go. He's not part of this."

"I'm afraid I can't do that. You see, he *is* part of this now." He leaned forward. "Do you know where your stepfather is?"

"Probably hiding. He must have known you were coming and took off. He's a coward." It hurt to talk about Sam like this, but I wanted Asim to think I was kind of on his side.

"Americans *are* cowards. They drop bombs from 30,000 feet and call it war. They kill women and children with their treaties and warfare."

Mr. Patterson gritted his teeth. "Our boys are the bravest fighters on the planet. And they don't tie up old men and kids in some basement."

Asim smiled. "So you know nothing about his whereabouts?"

"I know where he likes to go. A cabin not far from here."

"Where is it?"

"I can't explain. I'd have to take you there. Get me out of here and I'll show you. But you have to let Mr. Patterson go."

Asim stood and walked toward the shelves. "Bryce, this is not just about your father. It's about you, your family, your country, your way of life. It is fitting that we are in a school because I am your teacher. And I am very good at teaching."

"What are you going to do?"

"Has Sam told you what he did in my country?"

"He said he attacked the house he thought you were in."

"I wasn't there, but my family was. Your father and the men with him killed everyone. I promised my wife and children I would avenge their deaths. And I will."

I gulped. The way Asim talked, he could kill me in a second and not think twice.

He moved toward us, catlike and measured in his steps. "You believe you are safe, that your government protects you. You are wrong. Tomorrow your father and the whole world will learn a difficult lesson."

He leaned against a shelf, closed his eyes, and lifted his face to the ceiling. "Since you love your Scriptures, and since Christians love prophecy, we will fulfill one of old. 'A cry was heard in Ramah—weeping and great mourning. Rachel weeps for her children, refusing to be comforted, for they are dead.'"

I had heard those verses at our church in the past few months, but I couldn't place them. Ashley probably could because she's so good at memorizing.

"We've never done anything to you," Mr. Patterson said. "We live our lives and just try to get by. Now let this boy go—"

Asim backhanded him. "I should kill you now, but I will wait. I am your teacher, and I will show you what it means to suffer like we have." He looked back at me before he left. "And you are lying about the cabin and your stepfather."

CHAPTER 68

❀ Ashley ❀

"What's wrong?" Dylan said. He was finally picking up on Mom's fear.

"Just stay buckled, honey. We'll be okay." But I could tell by the look on her face that she didn't believe it.

"Let's go home," Leigh said. "Doesn't Dad keep a gun in the closet?"

"How did you know that?" Mom said.

"I've heard you talking."

"We're not going to lead them back there. Hang on." Mom turned left by a church and sped up. We dipped down, passing an office building, then zoomed up the other side. At the end of the street was a stop sign. Beyond that was the guardrail of I-25.

"Hang on!" Mom yelled, not even slowing down. She turned right, then jerked the wheel left, sending us careening into grass and dirt. My head nearly hit the roof, and I screamed. We banged over something. Then we were on I-25.

"How'd you know there was no fence there?" Leigh said.

"A good writer notices things," she said.

I looked back and saw that the car following us was stuck in the grass. "Let's call the police!" I said.

"No. Sam said not to get them involved."

"What?" Leigh said.

"He said to go somewhere safe, somewhere no one would think we would be."

"How about the alpaca farm?" I said.

"They might know the Morrises are our friends. No, it has to be almost a stranger." Mom took the next off-ramp and turned left toward the mountains.

That's when I figured out the perfect place to go.

CHAPTER 69

Bryce

Mr. Patterson finally cut through the hard plastic and got one hand free. He grabbed the blade, put it into the holder, and in a few seconds he had cut through the plastic holding my hands.

"We have to call the police," I said. "Where's the nearest phone?"

"In the classrooms, but if those are locked, we'll have to get to the front hall."

"Let's just run outside."

"I have a better idea. First thing we have to do is get you into the subbasement."

"What?"

"Follow me." He took me to the door leading to the subbasement.

"I don't want to go in there."

"I'm going to keep you safe until the police come." Mr. Patterson snatched a key taped under a shelf. "I put this here when you and your sister were locked in last year."

"But those guys have your keys," I protested. "You won't be keeping me safe."

"Bryce, I'd never forgive myself if those guys hurt you." He opened the door and turned on the light. "Go."

"What about you?"

He grabbed a huge pipe wrench. "Don't worry about me."

The door above us opened, and Mr. Patterson pushed me inside and closed the door. The key went in, the lock clicked, and something snapped. I guessed it was the key inside the lock—Mr. Patterson had broken it off. Then something banged on the handle. I heard yelling. At the fourth bang, something hit the floor. The doorknob!

Mr. Patterson had sealed me inside!

CHAPTER 70

❀ Ashley ❀

I gave Mom directions, and we pulled into the Heckler driveway. Bryce and I knew Boo and his family but not very well. The last time we were here, Boo's mom and dad were separated. Now there were two cars in the driveway.

We went to the front door, and Mom knocked lightly. A light was on upstairs and one at the back of the house. A cat sat in the window, and I recognized it as the kitten Boo had kept hidden in his barn. The cat looked healthy and happy sitting in the Hecklers' window.

A tall man who looked a lot like Boo opened the front door and looked at us through the screen. "Can I help you?"

"I'm Kathryn Timberline, and these are my children. Someone was following us. . . . It's actually a long story, but—"

"Are you Ashley?" Mr. Heckler said, looking past Mom.

I nodded. Leigh held Dylan in her arms.

"Come in. Come in," he said, opening the screen door. He had a slight drawl, just like Boo.

Mrs. Heckler turned on the living-room light and invited us to sit.

"Somebody was following you?" Mr. Heckler said.

"I can't explain everything," Mom said, "but my husband thinks we might be in danger."

"Oh, dear," Mrs. Heckler said.

While Mom talked, I looked down the hall and noticed a light on in Boo's room. I'd been here before and knew the layout.

"Can I get you something to drink?" Mrs. Heckler said.

"Root beer!" Dylan said.

Everybody laughed, and I followed Mrs. Heckler into the kitchen.

"I'm sorry you have to go through this," she said to me. "Where's your brother?"

"We can't find him," I said.

She hugged me, and I felt emotion bubble to the surface. I think she could tell because she tried to switch the subject. "You going to the dance next week?"

"I'm not sure. I had an invitation, but I haven't decided."

"Sounds kind of mysterious," she said. "What's up?"

I lowered my voice. "I've been getting notes, e-mails, and phone calls, but I can't tell who it is."

She put her hands on her hips and turned toward me. "He didn't sign it *Secret Admirer*, did he?"

My jaw dropped. "How did you know?"

One of the root beers overflowed, and she got some paper towels to clean up. As she wiped up the mess, she said, "One of the stories my kids love is about my husband's anonymous notes to me in high school. I wouldn't have given him the time of day otherwise, but those notes got to me."

I just stared at her, not knowing what to say.

"Aaron's acted strangely the past few days. I asked him about the dance, and he wouldn't say anything. Finally, your name came up. Said he didn't know if you would say yes or not."

My mind swirled like one of those vanilla/chocolate pudding pops. I had gone through the entire yearbook and had thought of Aaron but discounted him because his nickname Boo was in one of the letters.

"Would you like to talk with him?" Mrs. Heckler said.

I thought, *No, that's okay* and *Not in a million years.* But what came out was, "Yeah, sure."

CHAPTER 71

Bryce

I heard punching and moaning on the other side of the door. Asim yelled at the others to get the door opened, but their key wouldn't work.

"He's not going anywhere," another said.

"Drag this one upstairs," Asim said. "We'll deal with him there."

"Mr. Patterson?" I hollered.

With what sounded like his last ounce of strength, he said, "Remember what I told you. Back on that Sunday."

Then something banged, and I heard a dragging sound.

I slid down the door, thinking about Mr. Patterson. *What does he mean?*

I was thinking hard when something else popped into my head. The verse Asim had quoted. In our Christmas Eve service, little kids read the story of Jesus' birth. One read about King Herod ordering all male babies killed so he could get Jesus. That fulfilled a prophecy that said there would be weeping in Ramah.

The name clicked. The facts came together. Operation Hamar was no secret code—it was *Ramah* spelled backward. Ashley said her friend's assembly was at 10. Ours was at 9, the same time because of time zones. This was not just about Sam—it was a coordinated attack on schools!

Mr. Patterson's words came back to me, and I remembered the day he had let Ashley and me out of the subbasement. He told us how we could escape from it. I knew that's what I had to do.

CHAPTER 72

❀ Ashley ❀

I wasn't about to have a heart-to-heart with Aaron Heckler in front of my family, so I sat in a lawn chair on their back deck. My first run-in with Boo came last year, and it led to a huge confrontation. But in the past few months, Boo had changed. Bryce and I helped solve a case that got him released from juvenile detention. And I'd learned stuff about his past that made me feel sorry for him.

He came out the back door looking at the deck, his long arms swinging. He'd had a haircut since school got out.

"Hey," I said, waving.

"Hey," he said. As soon as he sat, he was up again and into the house. I thought it was the rudest thing I'd ever seen, but he returned with a book of matches and lit two candles that are supposed to keep mosquitoes away, even though we don't have mosquitoes.

The light flickered. He didn't look at me.

I took a deep breath. "So it was you."

"Yeah."

"Good disguise of your voice."

"Thanks."

"How'd you get the balloons in my locker?"

"Stuck them through the hole and then blew them up and tied them. Not that hard."

I watched the wax drip from the candles. "Why didn't you just come out and ask me?"

He snorted. "I knew you'd never go with me. You like that Duncan guy."

"How do you know that?"

He shrugged.

"You used your nickname in the note. How long have you known we call you Boo?"

"It's not a big secret. I thought it would throw you off."

"You were right." A pause. "I see your dad's back."

"Yeah, he and Mom are doing better, I think. They still fight sometimes because . . . well, my little sister . . ."

His little sister had been killed accidentally. "I know," I said. "I heard about what happened. I'll bet that was really hard."

He nodded. "Especially because it was my fault."

I edged a little closer. "That's not true, Aaron. Bad things happen. If you had been right there with her at the swings, you both would have been killed."

He looked at me. There was water in both our eyes. "I should have taken her with me across the street. I shouldn't have left her alone." He wiped his eyes with his sleeve. "There hasn't been a day that I haven't thought it should have been me instead of her."

"What happened to your sister was awful, but you can't blame yourself. I think God has a purpose for each of us."

"I don't like God very much."

"I felt that way after my dad died. I couldn't figure out why he'd let such an awful thing happen. But since then, God's become my friend. I think he wants to be your friend too."

Aaron wiped at his eyes again. "Maybe if you won't go to the dance with me, I can go to that youth-group thing."

I was about to speak when Mom rushed outside. "Ashley, we have to go. Mrs. Watson sees Bryce's ATV."

Aaron stood as Mom went back into the house. "I've never really talked to anybody about my sister," he said. "Thanks for listening."

I smiled and thought about Duncan, then about Bryce and Marion. The circle of love and all that. "Do you have any more roses?" I said.

"Why?"

"A girl should have flowers when she goes to a dance with her secret admirer."

CHAPTER 73

Bryce

I crawled up some shelves to inspect the metal vent running along the ceiling. Mr. Patterson had told Ashley and me that we could have escaped through this when we were trapped before.

I found a small hammer and used one end to unlatch an opening. I stuck the hammer in my pocket, stacked some boxes, and climbed inside the vent.

Great, no flashlight. What if I meet a rat or a raccoon in here? Or a snake?

I tried to push those thoughts away and started crawling.

CHAPTER 74

❀ Ashley ❀

I thought about Aaron all the way to Mrs. Watson's house. I figured one dance with the school's ex-bully wouldn't hurt. Besides, I looked forward to seeing people's faces when I walked in with him.

Mr. Heckler offered to drive us to Mrs. Watson's place, and Mom took him up on it.

Mrs. Watson came out in her nightgown and robe. Her hair was in curlers. She pointed at Bryce's ATV. "I didn't hear him drive up. Peanuts barked a few times, but he always does that."

Mom turned to me. "Where could he have gone?"

"He could have walked to the motel," I said.

"Then let's go back there and—"

Mom's cell phone rang. I could tell by the relief in her face that it was Sam. "Where are you?" she said. Pause. "We're at Mrs. Watson's place—his ATV is here. . . . No, Mr. Heckler drove us—Sam, somebody was following us after we left the motel. . . . Well, I couldn't leave him out here if—"

Sam cut her off and she nodded, taking his directions. She said, "Okay" a few times and hung up. "Could you take us back to our house so we can get some of our things?" she said to Mr. Heckler.

"Sure," he said.

CHAPTER 75

Bryce

Crawling on my hands and knees made too much noise, so I lay flat and pulled myself with my elbows. That was quieter. If you've ever seen those movies where somebody crawls through a clean vent with no dust or cobwebs, don't believe it. This was the dustiest place ever. And if I closed my eyes it couldn't have been any darker.

I crawled up an incline, then reached a steeper one. For that I put my feet on either side of the vent and pushed off. That led me to the main floor of the school. I came to a T and went right toward the office.

I moved faster, getting more excited about my escape. Then I heard someone shout. I could see through an opening below that Curly Hair and another guy were fighting, pointing fingers and yelling.

"He wants the young man now," Curly Hair said. "Get that door off!"

"But he will alert the people coming into the school."

"We will have his family. He will keep quiet if he knows we will kill them. Take the door off."

I waited for the two to leave, then continued. Mr. Patterson was nowhere in sight. The shaft snaked around a corner and into Mr. Bookman's office. I used the hammer to pry a vent loose, and it popped open, hanging by two small hinges. I put my head and shoulders through and fell. When I tried to grab the side, it cut my hand, and I landed with a thud.

Lights came on in the hall. I used the coatrack to close the vent just as a flashlight beam shot into the room.

CHAPTER 76

❀ Ashley ❀

It felt eerie going back into our dark house. Mr. Heckler had checked inside and gave us the go-ahead.

"Grab a suitcase and pack enough for a couple of days," Mom said.

"Where are we going?" Leigh said.

"Don't ask questions—just do it!" I'd never seen Mom so panicked. She went straight to her office and ripped out her laptop and threw all her thumb drives into a briefcase.

I grabbed my diary and a bunch of clothes and stuffed them into a duffel bag. Patches, my cat, mewed from under the bed, and I picked her up. On my dresser was a picture of Dad and me laughing at some crazy birthday party. He held me in his arms, twirling me. It was my favorite photo. I put it with my clothes and headed downstairs.

"Ashley, grab some of Bryce's things," Mom said.

I gave a sneer. "Underwear too?"

"Yes," she said. "Hurry."

I stopped on the stairs because something seemed weird. "Mom, what about Pippin and Frodo?"

CHAPTER 77

Bryce

I ducked the flashlight just in time and waited. When I was sure they had gone, I reached for Mr. Bookman's phone and punched 911. I held the phone to my ear and listened. Nothing but a buzz.

They must have cut all the phone lines, I thought.

The front window was small, but it was my best shot. I crawled to the wall and unlatched it. I moved books and files, and when I had a path cleared, I cranked the window open as far as I could.

Asim and another man walked into the secretary's office. I ducked and listened as they talked. I couldn't hear everything, but they said something about "the boy" and "the old man." I said a prayer for Mr. Patterson.

When they moved away, I rolled onto the window ledge and squeezed through the opening. It was tight, but I made it and dropped to the ground.

I scampered across the grass, a free man. I had escaped without anyone seeing me.

Except the guy in black who tackled me and threw me to the ground.

CHAPTER 78

❦ Ashley ❦

Mom's face scared me. As she grabbed Bryce's bag and told Leigh to hurry, I searched the house for our dogs. I called for them, whistling and clapping, but they didn't respond.

I moved outside and called again. The moon peeked through the clouds lighting up the red rocks behind our house. Had a fox or coyote grabbed them?

I found a flashlight in the barn and flicked it on. That's when I saw the white lump at the edge of the yard.

"Pippin!" I shouted. "Mom, come here!"

Pippin is older and moves a lot slower. Recently the vet had told us that Pippin might not be with us much longer, but I didn't believe it. He's so full of life. As I stood over his body, I prayed he would get up and bark. I put a hand to his head, and his body was cool. I jumped back as I found a red spot—dried blood—just behind his ear.

I screamed. The whole backyard was a blur.

Mom and Leigh ran outside.

"Who would do such a thing?" Mom gasped.

Leigh looked into the darkness. "Maybe they're still here."

CHAPTER 79

Bryce

I expected the guy in black to stick a gun in my face, but he didn't. He had dark green paint on his face and spoke into a microphone. "It's a kid, sir." He pulled me behind a pine tree.

Someone spoke into his earpiece.

"What's your name?" he said.

"Bryce Timberline."

"It's him, sir," the guy said.

Seconds later another guy in black ran toward us. He hugged me and I recognized Sam.

"Sam, it's him," I said. "Asim bin Asawe. He's come back for you."

"How many are inside?" Sam said.

"A bunch. At least four. Maybe more. Plus Mr. Patterson is in there. He saved my life."

Sam got on his radio and gave the info, though I couldn't understand what he was saying. It was like he was talking in some other language.

"Go to Mrs. Watson's house and stay there," Sam said.

"Wait, there are more of them at the motel."

"We've secured those rooms. They won't bother you anymore."

"But Operation Hamar—I figured it out."

That stopped him. "Go on."

"Asim quoted a verse—the one about Herod killing babies. It was in Ramah—that's Hamar spelled backward. I think these guys are going to hit schools tomorrow at nine our time."

The guy who tackled me raised his eyebrows. "We could've used him a few days ago, sir."

Sam smiled. "It was called the slaughter of the innocents. That's what these guys want to do. We're taking them down around the country—they'll be behind bars before anyone wakes up." He patted me on the shoulder. "You okay?"

For the first time I started to shake. "Yeah. Just be careful. I don't need to lose two dads to this guy."

"You won't," Sam said.

I took off across the field and reached my ATV. I sat there, studying the school.

A few seconds later the lights in the parking lot went out. Glass broke. Guns fired *pop-pop-pop*.

"Get him, Sam," I whispered.

CHAPTER 80

❀ Ashley ❀

I wanted to bury Pippin, but Mom said we didn't have time. Leigh cried as we wrapped him in the towel from his kennel and gently placed him near the house.

I wanted to say something profound, a poem or something, but all I could say was, "Good-bye, Pippin."

A motor revved in the distance, and Mom looked worried. "We have to leave—now!"

"No," I said, wiping away the tears. "That's Bryce's ATV!"

We hugged Bryce when he made it to the house. Then we broke the news about Pippin. He looked too stunned to cry. He told us what he'd seen at the school and that someone on Sam's team had told him to ride home.

Bryce grabbed his duffel bag and loaded it into Mr. Heckler's car. Dylan woke up just as we got in and cried for his blanket. Bryce said he knew where it was and went inside. As he passed the front porch, I heard something tinkling, like a wind chime—only smaller.

"Frodo," I whispered. Then I called him.

The little dog ran to the car and peed on the front tire before we could catch him. I put Patches in the back so they wouldn't fight. I still grieved Pippin, but having Frodo back took away some of the pain. Bryce brought out Dylan's blanket, and we drove to the Heckler house to get our car.

I didn't tell Bryce about Aaron because I wanted to wait for the right moment. Sometime in the future . . . like never!

We pulled into the driveway, got in our own car, and waited for Sam to call. Finally, we thanked the Hecklers and drove back toward town.

Suddenly, an explosion rocked the countryside, and a ball of fire rocketed skyward. It looked like the explosion was near the red rocks.

CHAPTER 81

Bryce

I prayed for Sam and Mr. Patterson and told everyone what had happened in the school. They couldn't believe I'd seen Asim bin Asawe. I hoped the school hadn't just blown up.

We drove toward the smoke and watched fire trucks and ambulances race ahead of us. I thought I saw a helicopter flying away from the area.

Mom's cell phone rang, and she pulled over. It was Sam asking where we were. She told him, and he said to stay there.

A few seconds later, a black object in the sky hovered over us, and

Sam slid down a rope dangling from a chopper. He jumped in the passenger side and told Mom to head for the interstate.

"What was that explosion?" I said.

He bit his lip. "We found out about their plan to attack the schools. They were going to do it at assemblies all around the country. We attacked them and blindsided them. But we can't be too careful at this point. We didn't get Asawe."

"What?" all of us said.

"I don't know how he got away, but he did. We got the rest of them."

"Wait, you blew up the school?" Ashley said.

"No." Sam pointed at the fire as we neared the on-ramp of the interstate. Because of our Christmas lights, every year we could pick out our house from this spot. Now there were only flashing lights and fire where our house had been.

"I don't understand," Leigh said.

"We're leaving Red Rock," Sam said.

We were all stunned. No good-byes. No hugging our friends and promising to write. We were leaving. End of story.

PART 4

CHAPTER 82

❦ Ashley ❦

When the sun came up, we were in Tacoma, Washington, refueling on a runway. Sam brought us a *USA Today*, and there was nothing inside about the school attacks.

"You won't be reading about the attacks," Sam said. "Nobody in the press knew about it, and all of the prisoners will be interrogated. This is one more secret you'll have to keep to yourselves."

"But what about the schools?" I said. "Won't you have to close them today to make sure?"

"A lot of them will be closed, yes."

"So what'll you tell the kids and parents? They'll want to know."

"Water leak. Something like that. We have all the targeted schools from a list Asawe made."

"What about the contest?"

"The contest was legit," Sam said. "These people just used it to get inside the schools."

"So we didn't win," Bryce said.

Mom looked in the mirror. "You're both winners."

I thought of all our friends back home. Marion Quidley wanted to be in our Bible study. Aaron Heckler wanted to take me to the dance. Would everyone think we'd died in the explosion? And what would happen to Mrs. Watson now that we were gone?

I had an appointment with the doctor in June, and he was supposed to say I could stop taking my seizure medicine. The nurses were planning a little party I'd been looking forward to for years.

Sam took off again, and we headed to an unknown destination. I got my diary out and wrote furiously in the back of the plane. Frodo sat on my lap most of the trip.

When we landed, it was hot and dry, but there were mountains in the distance.

Dylan wrapped his blanket around his arm and smiled. "It's just like Red Rock."

Bryce looked at me. "I don't think it'll ever be like Red Rock."

CHAPTER 83

Bryce

We read later that the body of the painter, Ernie, was found at the bottom of a ravine in Red Rock Canyon. The police had no suspects, but we knew Asawe's crew was responsible. Sam said they had probably stolen a local van so they wouldn't look suspicious.

We also found out through one of Sam's contacts that Mr. Patterson had survived. He had been wounded and spent some time in the hospital, but because of the blow to his head he couldn't remember what had happened. I think he knew exactly what happened and was keeping quiet.

Ashley moped around the next week. I think she was still wondering who her secret admirer was. Leigh went into a shell too, like a turtle pining for another lettuce leaf. I figured she missed Randy.

Mom stopped writing as Virginia Caldwell because it was too dangerous. The money she makes from her old books goes to the Chapman family, the people with the foster kids. I think that makes her happy, even though I see her typing sometimes in the middle of the night.

We had to break off all contact with our friends, which was hard. Sometimes I wish we could be back riding our ATVs and taking care of Amazing Grace and breathing the Colorado air, but you lose a lot when there are terrorists in the world.

I think about Boo and Duncan and Chuck and the others. I wonder if Marion Quidley thinks space aliens blew up our house, or if she started going to church and really believes in God. I hope she does. I also think about Mr. Bookman. And Mr. Forster, our old principal. And the people at the Toot Toot Café. And Lynette.

And Pippin.

That first week, Frodo sat near the window at our new house and looked out, as if he were waiting for his friend to return. From what Sam pieced together, two terrorists had gone to our house to capture us, and Pippin got in the way. Frodo ran through the electric fence and hid under the porch, but Pippin stood his ground.

We don't have many mementos of our old life in Red Rock, just a few pictures and a lot of memories. We did manage to get some mail. Someone from Sam's group intercepted it and delivered it a couple of months later. I was excited when I saw a letter sent by Mr. Elkins, the man whose wallet I found.

> Dear Bryce,
>
> I just wanted you to know what happened because of your kindness. I finally got up the courage to call Velma, and it was almost like we'd never been apart. I think we talked two

hours that first night. I flew out to see her the next weekend, and we had a good cry.

I asked her to marry me, and she accepted. I'm including an invitation to the wedding—we hope you'll accept and be our special guest. We'd like your whole family to come.

You never know what one act of kindness will do. Especially for a person you don't even know. I hope I get to meet you and thank you in person. If not, accept this letter as a token of thanks from someone whose life you've changed forever.

God bless you, Bryce. I hope to see you at the wedding.

Sincerely,
Pat Elkins

I looked at the date on the invitation. The wedding had already taken place, but the letter gave me a warm feeling. I had wondered if my life had made a difference to anyone in Red Rock. I wondered if anyone would remember the twins they knew back in middle school.

I guess that's what we all want to do—make a difference. Bloom where you're planted and all that. I just wish the blooming didn't have to hurt so much, but I guess that's life.

About the Authors

Jerry B. Jenkins (jerryjenkins.com) is the writer of the Left Behind series. He owns the Jerry B. Jenkins Christian Writers Guild, an organization dedicated to mentoring aspiring authors. Former vice president for publishing for the Moody Bible Institute of Chicago, he also served many years as editor of *Moody* magazine and is now Moody's writer-at-large.

His writing has appeared in publications as varied as *Reader's Digest*, *Parade*, *Guideposts*, in-flight magazines, and dozens of other periodicals. Jenkins's biographies include books with Billy Graham, Hank Aaron, Bill Gaither, Luis Palau, Walter Payton, Orel Hershiser, and Nolan Ryan, among many others. His books appear regularly on the *New York Times*, *USA Today*, *Wall Street Journal*, and *Publishers Weekly* best-seller lists.

Jerry is also the writer of the nationally syndicated sports story comic strip *Gil Thorp*, distributed to newspapers across the United States by Tribune Media Services.

Jerry and his wife, Dianna, live in Colorado and have three grown sons and three grandchildren.

Chris Fabry is a writer and broadcaster who lives in Colorado. He has written more than 40 books, including collaboration on the Left Behind: The Kids series.

You may have heard his voice on Focus on the Family, Moody Broadcasting, or Love Worth Finding. He has also written for Adventures in Odyssey and Radio Theatre.

Chris is a graduate of the W. Page Pitt School of Journalism at Marshall University in Huntington, West Virginia. He and his wife, Andrea, have been married 23 years and have nine children, two dogs, and one cat.

RED ROCK MYSTERIES

The entire series now available:

#1 Haunted Waters

#2 Stolen Secrets

#3 Missing Pieces

#4 Wild Rescue

#5 Grave Shadows

#6 Phantom Writer

#7 Double Fault

#8 Canyon Echoes

#9 Instant Menace

#10 Escaping Darkness

#11 Windy City Danger

#12 Hollywood Holdup

#13 Hidden Riches

#14 Wind Chill

#15 Dead End